MW01715866

As Time Goes By

Wendy Woods

CrossLink Publishing

As Time Goes By

CrossLink Publishing
www.crosslinkpublishing.com

ISBN 978-1-63357-005-4

Library of Congress Control Number: 2014949043

Scripture quotations are taken from the Holy Bible, King James Version (Public Domain).

Book Dedication

To Theresa Gloria Monaret Haydel and Noelle Woods:

My two purple-winged angels in Heaven

Chapter 1

The Approaching Season

Faith... what a complicated word to describe, especially since every single one of us has a different experience with it during our lifetime. The possible examples of faith are as endless as time. To some, faith is a rock, a fortress of beliefs which comforts and consoles. To others, it is something feared or questioned daily. How one views faith depends greatly upon how one views life. Is life a gift, or is life just something to be lost in time?

Bridget faltered between the two types of faith on a daily basis. She believed in God, but she wasn't convinced that he believed in her. Daily prayers fell on deaf ears. For ten years, God had been silent. Maybe Bridget preferred it that way. His silence meant that he neither loved nor despised her. Neutral was good. Neutral feelings prevented her heart from being ripped from her chest again. Feeling nothing was exactly how she wanted to live the rest of her life. But it was not to be.

Bridget's soul was like the calm before the storm. Her soul was still, quiet, and waiting to be electrified by something, anything. For ten long years, she had waited. Her wait was about to be over, but in a way that she never could have imagined. A spiritual storm was approaching. As the autumn wind blew through her hair, she wondered when the storms in her soul would pass. When would her morning come and would her soul ever see sunny skies again? Only Bridget and God knew the answer to that very question. This, my friends, is where Bridget's story begins…

A crisp, autumn breeze blew leaves of all colors around the back courtyard. It was Bridget's favorite time of the year. The children were playing in the backyard, jumping into piles of leaves, scattering them to the wind. It was a good thing that her uncle didn't mind the mess, or the company for that matter.

Bridget sipped her café au lait slowly and propped her feet up on the wrought iron chair. Paul sat across from her at the table and was laughing out loud at the kids' mischievous shenanigans. For a moment, he thought about joining in the fun until Bridget gave him the "I don't think so" look.

November had just begun, and Bridget was already halfheartedly looking forward to another holiday season. Thanksgiving and Christmas were her favorite times of the year, or so she liked to pretend. It was a time when families would reunite over tons of the best Cajun cooking. But it meant more to her than the social gatherings and delicious foods. It was a time for remembering. Despite the trials her family had faced through the years, Bridget was determined to make this the best holiday ever. She had to try her utmost for the sake of her family, and for her own sanity. Surely there was something worthwhile to cause rejoicing in her heart.

Paul could see that something was on her mind. "Penny for your thoughts, dear."

"You know me well, don't you?" she sighed. "I was thinking about the upcoming holidays and how much we need to make them special for the kids. Any ideas?"

Paul paused and gave her a worried look. "Bridget, you know we can't afford much this year. Your teacher's salary barely pays the bills. We can't count on my odd and end jobs to provide for luxuries such as Christmas gifts. The kids will just have to understand that this year they may have to go without some of the things they want. I'm sorry, but with no steady work in the near future, I'm afraid there are no other options. And before you even suggest the idea, as you always do, we are not accepting money from your uncle."

"I hadn't planned on asking Uncle Sidney for money, but you know he's going to insist that we take enough to buy the kids gifts for Christmas. And, I know how you feel about taking money from him or anyone else, honestly I do. However, you do need to come to the realization that he's my grandmother's only brother. He has the money, and all his life he's done nothing but help others. Uncle Sidney can't help the fact that he has a generous heart, especially when it comes to me. And, it's not like we don't do anything in return for his generosity. Who cooks every night and cleans the house for him? Don't you make repairs, mow the property, and clean the stalls in the barn?"

"Well, yes, we do help out around here, and I know Sidney is grateful. I don't mean to harp on things, but it's bad enough we have to live here with him and depend on him to take care of my own family. I feel so useless."

Paul was beyond frustrated. He had been laid off for almost six months from the construction job at the refinery. He had worked for the Lyon Construction Company since he graduated high school. With nothing beyond a high school diploma, Paul's options were limited. Times were tough, and the economy prevented many businesses from hiring skilled labor. The sugar refinery project had been scaled back and put on hold until the company could come up with more funding for the upgrades. Since then, he had picked up short term jobs here and there, doing pretty much anything to make ends meet. At times, he regretted the fact that he hadn't gone on to college like Bridget and his brother, Peter. The thought, however, faded as he admitted to himself that working with his hands and being outdoors had always made him happy. A desk job would kill him for sure, more than his current unemployment.

Bridget's teacher salary had been the only thing that prevented them from going into total bankruptcy. Luckily, they still had Bridget's state health insurance and her retirement to fall back on if needed. And, of course, Uncle Sidney had come to their rescue. After Paul and Bridget had to sell their home, Sidney insisted that the family move into his home. He wondered why they hadn't asked for the money to pay their mortgage note.

The relocation to Uncle Sidney's home was a blessing, even though Paul did not care to admit it. His house was a large, brick colonial built during the late 1800's. It had been in his wife's family for hundreds of years. As a wedding gift, Esther inherited the home from her parents. The home hadn't changed much since it was built. The bricks remained an off white color, offset by the darkest hunter green shutters. A huge porch wrapped around the entire back of the house and was surrounded by a beautiful brick courtyard with a huge sugar kettle fountain in the center. Sidney and Esther had lived in the home for decades. They took years renovating the house to its original grandeur, along with the gardens and stables. The house became their pride and joy. And with all the extra room in such a large estate, it wasn't uncommon for them to invite friends and family over to stay on for weeks at a time to visit.

Yes, the house had supplied them with many years of joy and happy memories, except for one. The footsteps and laughter of children were never a blessing that God granted to them…a sound that would never be heard on the staircase or in the courtyard or stables. It took years for Esther to come to terms with her fate. But the birth of her first niece, Bridget, gave her an unexplained joy and a reason to live. Bridget became like a daughter to Esther and Sidney. They spoiled her beyond measure, until the other nieces and nephews came into the family. Their wealth of attention then had to be shared, but Bridget always knew she would forever be their favorite little girl.

It had been almost a year since Esther had passed. After her death, the house felt empty and left Sidney longing for companionship. Bridget would check on her uncle daily, afraid that he would not be able to survive without Esther. So, when Bridget and Paul lost their home, it was only natural that they move in with Sidney. The house came alive once again, and Sidney could barely stand it when they all left for school or work. He would waste time at the local hardware store, barber shop, or diner just to keep from missing them so much. It was a temporary arrangement, but Sidney secretly wished that they would stay forever.

Bridget stood up and hugged Paul's neck. "Honey, I know you hate asking for help. This hasn't been easy on any of us. But, you'll get back on the job again. And you aren't useless to us. We love you and need you now more than ever. So what if you aren't bringing in a lot of money right now? We will make due with what we've been given. Besides, you need to look at it this way. I was spending half my days here checking on my uncle. You know how much I worried over how he was going to make it without my aunt. Now I can watch over him all the time. We are like a tonic for him. He loves us all so much, in a sense, he needs us more than we need him."

Paul laughed under his breath, "I suppose you have a point. I just hate not being able to give you and the kids everything you want and then some."

Bridget kissed him on the cheek, "You old fool. You are all I need. Fate will take care of the rest. So, let's relax and enjoy the weeks ahead. I'm sure the kids will appreciate whatever they receive. After all, it's the time you spend, not the money you spend that matters in the end."

Paul gave her hands a squeeze. "You know why I love you so much?"

Bridget giggled, "Because I'm so much smarter than you are?"

"Funny." He grabbed her by the arms and sat her down on his lap. "Nope, it's because you always know how to make me feel better. You have a way of looking at things so differently than I do. How about we start getting the lights down out of the attic this afternoon? It'll take us a month to decorate Sidney's yard!"

And with that, Bridget took off running from the courtyard, into the house, and up the stairs to the attic faster than Paul could catch up to her. The holiday spirit was about to descend upon the house. Bridget needed the Christmas spirit more than anyone, only she was better at hiding it.

Chapter 2
Dark Clouds on the Horizon

The next few weeks leading up to Thanksgiving were bustling and extra busy. Bridget had spent countless hours on the internet planning fun lessons and art projects for the students in her classroom to keep their little minds busy. She knew idle kids meant trouble, especially with the excitement of the holidays approaching. She had also picked up a few kids to tutor two days a week after school, which meant a little extra cash for Christmas.

Paul had managed to find a part-time job at the local nursery. They needed some extra hands unloading fresh Christmas trees and all the decorations that went along with the season. It wasn't a great paying job, but it was money. And he was more than grateful for it.

The children, Eli and Grace, were busy each afternoon practicing at the church for the upcoming Christmas pageant. Eli had nominated Uncle Sidney to help paint the props on stage, along with several other men in the congregation. Sidney couldn't have been more thrilled with the invitation, so he took charge of the children in the afternoons until Bridget and Paul made it home.

Over dinner one night, they discussed the preparations that needed to be made before Thanksgiving Day. A long grocery list began to form as Uncle Sidney kept adding more and more items to the menu. Bridget laughed and told him he was going to have enough food to feed the Army! He insisted though, knowing most of the family would be there for dinner. Even the relatives from north Louisiana were going to make it down this year. It was going to be a grand feast indeed.

Finally, the week of Thanksgiving had arrived. Bridget and the children were off of school for the holiday. Bridget could finally get a few things accomplished, like hemming Grace's angel costume for the pageant, writing out Christmas cards, and reading the last few chapters of a novel she had started since September. There was so much to do, her mind raced.

Even though this was a joyous time, it was a bit overwhelming with all of the expectations set before her. As much as she loved the holidays, she also dreaded them just the same. Sometimes she would rather run away from it all and call it a season for forgetting. Was it really worth all the hassle and the stress? She often wondered if anyone else felt the same, or if something deep down inside was wrong with her. Of course, if anyone had reason to want to forget the season, it was Bridget.

Bridget's thoughts about the week's agenda were interrupted when her cell phone rang. It was her mother. "Hey mom, are you calling to see what Sidney wants us to make for Thanksgiving dinner? If so, you better get over here now, because it will take a week to fix it all!"

Her mother let out a chuckle. "Ah, my uncle always has a mountain of food, doesn't he? Well, let me know what day you want to hit the grocery store for everything. I'll come help you with the shopping. I'm fixing to go down to the church and hem some of the kids' pageant costumes. Do you need me to work on Grace's for you?"

"Nope, I think I'll work on it tonight, but thanks anyway. We can shop tomorrow. I'll pick you up around nine." As they hung up, Bridget almost regretted not letting her mother hem Grace's costume. With so much to do, she'd have to make time to tend to the task. Her mother had enough to do anyway.

Bridget went into the office and picked up the novel she was dying to finish, as well as a stack of Christmas cards. She headed to the back porch swing and sat in the afternoon sunshine. The kids had run outside to romp in the yard before the expected storms would move in later. The kids were playing in the barn with the horses, chickens, and the goats. Why her uncle needed such animals was beyond her comprehension. Sidney used the excuse that they would make great fair exhibits for the children, and when Eli joined the 4-H club next year, the livestock would be readily fattened for showing. In all honesty, Sidney enjoyed the animals just as much, if not more, than the children.

The peace and quiet of the afternoon allowed Bridget to finish off the novel and make a good dent in the pile of cards to write. She closed her eyes for a few minutes, as a familiar Christmas song played in the background. The radio station had already begun playing holiday music non-stop.

Her mind then drifted to earlier days during her marriage to Paul. Life had been so simple before…Bridget couldn't finish the thought. Had he forgotten ten holidays ago? Had he blocked that time out of his mind just to be able to exist from day to day? Why had life moved on so easily and effortlessly for him and not for her? How had his faith in God stayed so strong when hers did nothing but falter daily for over ten years?

At that moment, she spoke to God. "Lord, what's wrong with me? Why can't I get over this hurt? Life is moving on without me. I am so lost. Maybe I want to stay lost to dull the pain. Help me this holiday season. Help me to rejoice again, Lord." Tears fell down her cheeks. She quickly wiped them away as Eli and Grace came running toward her.

"The animals are all fed, Mom," Eli informed her. "The chickens are getting kinda spooked. I think they know a big storm is coming."

"I think you are right, son. Animals have a sense about these things."

"Mamma, do you think the horses, chickens, and goats will be safe in the barn tonight?" Grace's love for animals was always apparent in her gentle ways and compassion toward them.

"Yes dear, the animals will be fine in the barn. So, don't you worry. The storm will be over by morning. It's just a cold front moving through just in time for Thanksgiving." She hugged Grace and told them both to wash up for dinner.

As she picked up her things from the swing, Bridget could see dark blue clouds moving in on the horizon. A steady breeze began to blow all around her. The storm would be there within the hour, just as Paul would be arriving home from the nursery and Sidney from the barber shop. Her family would be safe and warm, too.

A weather bulletin came across the radio announcing severe thunderstorms were on the way. The announcer stated strong winds, heavy rain, and dangerous lightning were possible. The storm would continue through the night, then sunny skies would return by morning.

Before Bridget turned off the radio, she stopped and looked once more at the ominous clouds thundering in the distance. It was exhilarating watching the lightning flash across the sky. If only a tiny spark would ignite her spirits this season. It was a time for miracles, or so she had heard. Bridget, however, wasn't the least bit convinced.

Chapter 3

HOLIDAY BLUES

Bridget's holiday blues had haunted her for ten years. She had good cause to hate the holiday season. Every year she dreaded these weeks, wondering what new horrific event could possibly take place during what was supposed to be such a joyous season. Crowds of festive, happy people made her nauseous. What were they so happy about?

Bridget found no reason to celebrate. She only pretended to enjoy the season and hid her true feelings so well with fake smiles that not even Paul suspected a thing was wrong. It was pointless to confront him. He would never understand why she had held onto these feelings for nearly a decade. He would probably tell her she needed to forget it and move on, as he had done long ago.

Memories of the past rushed out of her thoughts as soon as her mother arrived at the house that Wednesday morning to begin the Thanksgiving preparations. She had to put on a good face for her mother. After all, her mother had to be feeling a little blue too. It had only been six months since Bridget's grandmother, Gloria, had passed away. Surely this holiday season was going to be hard on her mother. The loss of her grandmother only added to Bridget's building resentment for the season.

The kitchen soon filled with wonderful aromas from the oven. Bridget and her mother were icing a red velvet cake. "This was your maw-maw's favorite holiday cake." Her mother sighed deeply, "She had the best recipe in town. As hard as I try, I just can't get the icing to taste the same. Maybe there was something she never…" tears ran down her mother's face, "she never told me to put in it. Oh Bridget, I miss her so much!"

Bridget immediately comforted her mother, although she wasn't much help. She began crying, remembering years of holidays gone by.

"Her secret ingredient was probably whiskey!" Bridget got tickled through the tears. "You know she would never admit she put a shot of the stuff in her fudge, but I think we all know she did it."

Bridget's mother smiled at the thought. "You are so right. Gloria was something, wasn't she? Maybe we should try a shot in the icing and see if that's the trick."

"Nah, if we are going to open that bottle of whiskey, it won't be for cake icing, I assure you!"

The rest of the day, Bridget and her mother talked about the good holiday memories they had shared with Gloria. It was therapeutic for both of them in many ways. Gloria might be gone, but she would not be forgotten. She would celebrate Thanksgiving with them, if only in memory.

That evening, Bridget had settled into a hot bubble bath to relax before the craziness of Thanksgiving Day fell upon the house come morning. Her eyelids felt heavy and began to close. Her mind drifted back to the conversation she had with her mother earlier that day. Her grandmother's life weighed heavily on her mind.

Before she knew it, her dreams took her back to the ICU with her mother and sister. It had been the longest week of their lives. Gloria's health had faded for months, and they were not surprised by yet another trip to the hospital. It had been her third trip in less than two months. Every time the family thought the end was near, Gloria would make an amazing recovery and snap back to her old self. So, this ICU stay hadn't concerned them much at first.

Gloria had spent a few days perfectly coherent, asking for gumbo and wedding cake of all things! She laughed at jokes, made small talk with the family, and knew every visitor by name. It was surprising to Bridget when she got a call from her mother urging her to come to the hospital. Gloria was fading quickly. Within 48 hours, her body began to shut down. Her speech was limited to slurs and nods. The ICU nurse had informed them that it would be a matter of hours, not days, when she would pass on.

Bridget's mother, Ann, took the news hard. She almost drifted into denial until Bridget and her sister, Elizabeth, intervened. "Mamma, you have to let her go," Elizabeth coaxed. "She's in pain and her body isn't able to heal itself any longer. She'll be better off in Heaven where she will be free of pain and suffering."

Elizabeth was a nurse, and she had comforted many families in her line of work. She handled things so delicately without falling apart. Bridget admired her strength and compassion.

Their mother refused to let Gloria go. Sidney had faced the reality of his sister's condition and had come to terms with the inevitable. He begged Bridget to talk some sense into Ann.

Another twenty-four hours passed, and it was time to make a life altering decision. Should Gloria be put on life support or resuscitated when her body could no longer survive on its own? Ann knew doing so would go against her mother's wishes, and deep down she didn't want to prolong her mother's suffering. But how could she let go?

As Bridget and Elizabeth walked into the room, Ann was apologizing for all the things she felt she had done wrong, begging for her mother's understanding and forgiveness.

The sight of it made Bridget jump into action. She couldn't bear seeing her mother suffering and easing her conscience, which was right as rain. None of that mattered now. All wrongs were righted and all things forgiven. Gloria had to die in peace, and Ann had to let her.

"Mamma, it's time." Bridget hugged her mother. Tears flowed from all of the faces in the room. "Mamma, she won't go until you tell her it's alright to leave. She needs to know you will be okay without her. Tell her she has no unfinished business on Earth. Please tell her it's time for her to meet Jesus and to fly with the angels she's been seeing."

Earlier in the week, Gloria had mentioned seeing her deceased parents, in addition to, angels all around her in the ICU room. She had spent countless hours gazing at the ceiling as if someone was there with her. When Ann asked if she still saw angels, a simple nod was given. Bridget even lightened the mood by asking what color angel wings Gloria wanted in Heaven. She named every color in the book. When purple was mentioned, a giggle and a smile spread across Gloria's face. Purple wings it would be.

Ann held back her tears. "Mamma, you can go now. I'll be alright. We will all be alright. Go home. Go home to Jesus. We will miss you. Just save us a place when you get there. Go home."

And with Ann's permission, Gloria took her last breath and flew on to Heaven, wearing the most beautiful purple wings.

Bridget was suddenly awakened by a knock on the bathroom door. "You okay in there?" Paul beckoned.

"I'm fine. I must have fallen asleep. I'll be out in a minute." She quickly dried off and was grateful such a dream was over. "Holidays suck," she muttered to herself. "Lord, give me strength to survive another year. Help me with the holiday blues."

Chapter 4

Thanksgiving Again

Thanksgiving morning arrived with an unusual chill in the air. Everyone in the house was bustling with excitement about the day's events. Bridget quickly got dressed in jeans and a warm sweater and headed downstairs. Sidney and Paul were in the kitchen drinking coffee and teasing the kids about the annual family football game. They were telling the kids strategies for cheating, of course. Bridget thought for a moment about scolding the two instigators, but she knew it would be a futile effort.

As soon as Bridget's parents arrived, everyone was shooed out of the kitchen so that Ann and Bridget could get lunch ready for the impending crowd. As noon approached, relatives began appearing with armfuls of traditional holiday dishes. By one o'clock, everyone had settled down at the table to eat. Sidney said a quick blessing of thanks. Then, the noise commenced as dishes clanged and lively conversations continued.

After lunch was devoured and the men had caught an afternoon nap or the tail end of the Saints game, it was time for the annual slaughtering of one unlucky team. Oh, there were no rules, so cheating and name calling was to be expected. The ladies of the family, being the smarter sex, decided to spend their afternoon on the courtyard sipping coffee and catching up on the latest family gossip.

Bridget loved listening to the stories of times gone by as the older ladies reminisced about holidays past. Great-aunt Mabel's stories about the Great Depression and World War II times were Bridget's favorite. Her tales always included Gloria, so naturally it held Bridget's interest. Bridget had always felt as though she belonged in a different time era, and Aunt Mabel's stories only brought the eras to life.

The peaceful courtyard retreat was suddenly invaded by the victorious team. All of the men and children brought their cheers and ruckus onto the courtyard. Bridget retreated into the kitchen to refill her coffee and to get away from all the merriment for a moment. She grabbed her phone and scanned her messages from well-wishing friends and posted a few pictures on Facebook of the day's events.

"I suppose this is another Thanksgiving come and gone." She mumbled to herself and sighed. As she scrolled through some photos, she came across a photo of Gloria. "Oh, maw-maw, I wish you were here. I wish Noelle was here, too. Hope the two of you are keeping each other company. I'm jealous, you know. You have her, and I…I don't!" She began sobbing uncontrollably.

The back porch door swung open and Bridget quickly wiped away her tears and put on a fake smile. Paul had ventured inside to check on her. He had no clue just how hard holidays were for her. And Bridget had no intention of ever letting him know that fact.

"Hey honey. We are all about ready to turn on the Christmas lights for the kids to see before everyone heads home. I know you don't want to miss it. Sidney already has the family rounded up like cattle, waiting for the flick of the switch. I think he's just waiting to start his usual singing of Christmas carols, as off key as they are! You coming?"

"Yes, I'm coming. Let me put this cup in the sink. I'll be right there."

As soon as Bridget stepped out onto the courtyard, Sidney and the kids began doing a countdown from ten. At one, the switch was flipped and the entire courtyard and front of the house blazed forth in Christmas glory. Twinkle lights in every color illuminated the exterior of the house. Bridget thought to herself that Paul had really outdone himself this year. Apparently, he had done much more decorating than she realized. The family was mesmerized by the sight. Sidney led the caroling with a lively rendition of "Jingle Bells." After caroling came to an end, everyone packed up and headed home. Bridget waved goodbye to the last family leaving the driveway. She was alone. She took in the lights around her as the cold night air gave her a chill. She looked up to the star filled sky.

"Fa-la-la-la-la-la-la-la-blah!"

And with that she slammed the door shut to more than just the cold night air and happy holiday decorations. And she knew it, but she really didn't care.

Chapter 5

Blue Christmas

The weeks leading up to Christmas were busy as expected. Holiday parties, church functions, and shopping were all enough to keep Bridget's mind occupied. The last day of school before Christmas break had arrived, and every one of her students was bursting with anticipation for Santa's arrival in a few days. Bridget delighted in their innocent faith and secretly wished she could have that same child-like belief in something…anything.

Maybe this would be the year she would let go of the past and live in the present. Her heart had hardened so much through the years with blame, guilt, and despair. How could she find her way back to her former self? Where had the devoted, faithful person gone for ten years? And why, after all these years, would God want her back?

But, she couldn't think of that now. Grace's big performance as an angel and Eli as a shepherd was tonight at the church, and she had to hurry home to make the finishing touches on her daughter's costume. Bridget grabbed her purse and keys, locked her classroom door, and headed for home.

She was no sooner on the highway when her cell phone rang. "Hello?"

"Hey honey, before you head home, can you swing by the nursery? Father John picked two trees out for the play tonight. Since you have the truck today, I told him you wouldn't mind dropping those to him at the church."

"Sure, I'll be there in five minutes." Bridget hung up the phone and gritted her teeth. She didn't need any more interruptions in her day. She had things to do and wanted a little down time to herself before all the holiday obligations began.

The nursery was packed full of shoppers trying to pick out the perfect Christmas tree. Bridget always wondered why some people procrastinated so long to buy a tree. Her tree had been trimmed the weekend after Thanksgiving. To each his own, she grimaced to herself.

She found Paul and had the trees loaded into the truck. He kissed her goodbye and told her that he would meet her at the church at six. Bridget cranked the truck and sped down the highway to the church. Christmas carols blared from the radio. Elvis was belting out "Blue Christmas."

"Enough of this torturous music!" She pushed a CD into the player and waited for something more soothing than lousy Christmas carols to play. As luck would have it, one of her favorite tunes from the Depression era played softly. Bridget sang along to "As Time Goes By," which was one of Gloria's favorites from the era and a song from their favorite movie, *Casablanca.* She could recall a time that her grandmother had rejoiced at hearing Louis Armstrong belt out that song again. Bridget had spent countless hours downloading music onto a CD as a special surprise for Gloria. Swing, jazz, GI blues, and songs of her youth were all there for her listening pleasure. After all, time passed slowly at the nursing home, so anything to occupy the hours was appreciated.

Bridget pulled into the church parking lot and went into the church hall to find Father John. She soon found two willing helpers to bring the trees inside for display. Father thanked her for the delivery. It was just the two of them for what felt like days. For years, Bridget had wanted to confess all her doubts and fears to the good priest, hoping he could bring her back to God, but the timing never seemed right. Today was no exception, as tempting as it might be. Father John was far too busy with the task at hand to worry over a mere lost soul.

Bridget hurried back to the truck, heart heavy with the burden that she had carried for so long, but she was far too busy to concern herself with her own problems at the moment. She had to hurry home, for other, more important things took precedence over her estranged relationship with God.

The afternoon sped by in a whirlwind as Bridget mended Grace's costume, baked cookies for the church party, ironed outfits for her family, and cleaned up the kitchen. Bridget never found that desired down time she craved. Like a good mother, she just kept going. She would sleep late in the morning and relax after tonight. It was just another day in the life of Bridget.

The Christmas play was adorable. The family delighted in the performance, especially Grace's role as an angel and Eli's role as a shepherd. Grace had a speaking part, while Eli tended to the live animals on stage. Uncle Sidney, of course, had loaned out his prize goat, which kept making a ruckus during the songs. The crowd laughed as the old goat appeared to be making an attempt to sing along.

During the party in the church hall, Bridget found herself face to face with Father John. He commented on how wonderful the program had turned out. He inquired about holiday plans and Paul's luck at finding steady work. However, something more was on his mind. He hesitated before continuing.

"Bridget, I had a feeling earlier today that you wanted to talk to me about something important. You know, I do have time for you after the holidays if you want to schedule an appointment."

Bridget suddenly felt a rush of heat over her body. "Thank you, Father John. I appreciate the offer. I'm fine, really. It's nothing. Just preoccupied with the holidays ahead, that's all."

"Okay, if you say so dear. Just know I'm available if and when you need me. I'll be visiting family up around Monroe after Christmas services. I'll be there a week, but I do have a good friend of mine that will be taking my place. Perhaps he could be of assistance during my vacation, if needed. If you'll excuse me, I must help Santa to his chair. I see Sister Margaret is trying to keep Santa from being bombarded by the children. Have a Merry Christmas!"

Bridget thanked him for his concern and wished him a happy holiday season. Was it that obvious that she longed to spill out her soul? For a brief moment, the thought of talking to a complete, unbiased stranger was appeasing. At least she could sit in church knowing that Father John did not know her secrets. Then again, she rarely sat in church these days anyway. Paul and the children remained loyal churchgoers. But with time and separation, Bridget found it easier to just stay away from the whole holier than thou façade and attended church only when the need arose. Why pretend?

Oh, she believed in Heaven and Hell and in God and the devil. Believing wasn't the problem at all. Bridget and her family had seen God's great, majestic creation on a trip to the Smoky Mountains many years ago. If she ever doubted his existence, the beauty all around her convinced her otherwise. And Bridget had seen the devil's work in many ways through the years. The evils of the world around her made their presence known through the eyes of abused children, hate crimes, war, and so on. The devil came in and out of her life, causing doubt, rejection, and apathy. But even Satan wasn't Bridget's major problem. Nope, he couldn't take credit for the ten years of turmoil since Noelle's death.

A battle raged within Bridget. The worst enemy whom she faced was herself alone.

Chapter 6

Christmas, Here We Come

It was Christmas Eve. Bridget and Paul still had shopping to do for Santa's arrival. It was the latest Bridget could remember shopping for gifts. The tree this year looked so lonesome. Only a few boxes circled its lower branches. She managed to pick up a few cheap items at the dollar store in town to exchange on Christmas Eve. It was their family tradition to choose one gift to open from under the tree. Bridget only hoped that the trinkets that she had managed to buy would be enough to delight the children. After all, there was little more than one hundred dollars left after paying the bills.

Paul was free for the afternoon. With his last paycheck from the nursery in hand, along with some cash Bridget earned during after school tutoring, they headed for the stores. Paul told Bridget that the nursery manager offered him part-time work in the spring. It wasn't much, but at least it was a promise of some kind of work.

Paul and Bridget discussed getting the children new bikes. Grace wanted a Barbie doll and a horse stuffed animal. Eli wanted a monster truck and a Star Wars action figure. Thankfully, their lists weren't lengthy, and whatever Santa brought would thrill them on

Christmas morning. It also helped that Bridget's best friend, Evelyn, worked at the store and offered them her discount to help cover the cost of the toys. As much as she hated accepting the offer, there really was not another option beyond a handout. Paul had already adamantly declined any help from Uncle Sidney or their parents.

As they approached the store front, Bridget noticed cages of dogs and cats lining the sidewalk. The local animal shelter was making one last attempt to get the remaining animals adopted before the holidays.

"Paul, look at those cute puppies! Awe, I bet the kids would love a dog, don't you think?" She approached the kennels and scanned over the puppies.

"Don't even get attached. You are about as bad as your uncle with animals. You would bring home the entire shelter if I let you. Now, let's get what we came in here for before everything is gone. Christmas, here we come!" Paul eased her away from the barking fur balls, and they continued into the store.

An hour later, and twenty bucks left in their pockets, the couple pushed the buggy towards the exit. The animal shelter was still outside. A sign advertised a holiday special: Adopt one pet, get another free! Bridget pointed the sign out to Paul. Only a few animals remained, and it was clear that the shelter workers were on a mission to get all the animals good homes.

Paul gave Bridget a look. "Come on honey, we don't need to even look at the dogs and cats left. We don't have enough money to adopt one, much less get shots and vet care right now."

Bridget sadly looked away. A shelter volunteer had overheard the conversation. "Excuse me folks, would you be interested in taking home a great pet for Christmas? All of our cats and dogs are very sweet and have all their first year shots up to date and are fixed, so no vet bills to worry over for a year. It's a good deal today, two pets for one low price!"

Bridget gave Paul a weary look, as her eyes begged him to listen. He never could tell her no very often. "Well, that all sounds fine and well, but I'm afraid we have twenty bucks left to our name, so I'm sure that won't cover the adoption fee. Sorry Bridget, but we don't have the money. Maybe in the spring we can look again."

The volunteer piped up and smiled she gave a wink to Bridget. "Actually, you are in luck. We are also offering half off our usual adoption fee. Twenty bucks will cover everything. Plus you can adopt another pet if you like. It's a win-win really for you and the animals. So, what do you think guys? Would you like to pick out a new family member?"

Bridget pleaded, "Please Paul, please let's do it. The kids would be so surprised by a dog! You know how much Grace loves animals. And all boys need a good dog. Eli would love it! And I get paid in a week. We can manage til then."

Paul sighed. "It's pointless to argue with you, isn't it? Go ahead. But no puppies or kittens. Get an older animal that's housebroken. Winter is a horrible time to train a pet. And think of your uncle having to tend to it while we are gone all day."

Bridget practically jumped into his arms. "Thank you, honey! Oh, the kids will love this!" Bridget scanned the remaining dogs and cats. She instantly fell in love with a three year old Australian Shepherd. She would make a good watchdog and playmate. Paul agreed the dog was a good choice.

As Paul filled out the adoption papers, Bridget noticed that only two cats remained. She saw an orange tomcat that meowed at her as she bent in for a closer look. He was fat and friendly. He reminded her of Garfield. Then, a thought popped into to her head. She hadn't bought Uncle Sidney a gift. She recalled hearing him say on several occasions that a good tomcat would be a big help in the barn to keep mice and snakes away. And since they were adopting the dog, the cat would go home for free.

Bridget discussed her idea with Paul. Soon enough, they were heading back home with gifts to wrap and two animals to hide. Bridget thought to herself, maybe this was going to be a great Christmas after all. A day of happiness and joy is just what her heart and soul needed.

As they arrived home, Bridget quickly unloaded the few gifts and went straight to wrapping. Paul took the animals into the barn and made them a warm stall filled with hay. Time was of the essence. Ann had agreed to make cookies with Eli and Grace at her house until it was time for church.

Christmas Eve mass went on as usual, and Bridget sat and listened to the sermon and choir hymns as she always had each year. She was no more moved or motivated to change her life or faith. She looked at her watch, counting the minutes until it was all over so that her family could get home to begin their Christmas Eve traditions.

Back home at last, everyone shed their Christmas best and slipped into comfortable clothing for the night's festivities. For years, Uncle Sidney had hosted a huge bonfire party with family and friends. Anyone in town could venture over to the house, for Sidney was a most generous and gracious host. His only stipulation was to bring a dish to share. It saved Bridget and Ann from having to cook two days in a row. They were thankful for his insight. Through the years, they had also talked him into renting tents and tables for the courtyard to host his guests. The days of midnight cleaning in the house were well over. The mess could stay outside until after Christmas Day, and Bridget and Ann were more than ecstatic about it.

Before the party began, Bridget, Paul, and the children sat around the Christmas tree. Eli and Grace chose one gift to open. After unwrapping a toy cap gun and a light up princess wand, the children ran around the house, pretending and testing out their new trinkets. Apparently they were a hit, so Bridget was relieved. Her thoughts were soon interrupted by the doorbell. Guests were beginning to arrive and it was time to play hostess and visit with dear family and friends.

The party began winding down around ten o'clock, as families headed home to play Santa or to turn in for the night. Shortly before midnight, Bridget and Paul quietly snuck downstairs with gifts in hand and laid them beside the tree. Santa had arrived! They joked about seeing the looks on the kids' faces once the dog and cat were introduced. They plotted and came up with an idea to leave Eli and Grace a note from Santa. Bridget wrote careful clues in the note that would lead the children to the barn. She couldn't wait until morning and found it hard to fall asleep.

Morning arrived with screams of excitement as the children ran downstairs. Bridget and Paul rolled out of bed and met the children by the tree. Uncle Sidney already had coffee brewing and cinnamon rolls in the oven. Wrapping paper and bows were thrown everywhere as the children dove into their gifts from Santa. A note from Santa was found inside Eli's stocking. The children put on their coats and invited Uncle Sidney to help them uncover the clues.

As they were led to the barn, Bridget and Paul could hardly contain their excitement. Suddenly, the Aussie began to bark wildly. The children ran to the stall to discover their special gift. The dog barked and jumped all over the children. She was so happy to finally be free and loved. The cat, not to be outdone, began meowing. Bridget scooped him up and handed him to her uncle.

"Merry Christmas! You said you needed a good tomcat for the barn, so here he is! Santa wanted you to have a cat. Hope you like him." She patted the cat's soft fur.

"Well, isn't that something! Look kids, I have a new friend too! Boy, Santa sure knew we needed a cat and a dog, didn't he kids?" The kids laughed as they rolled around in the hay with their new best friend.

Lunch was a lively event. Bridget's sister, Elizabeth, along with several cousins, aunts, and uncles showed up with their families. It was a smaller gathering than Thanksgiving, but the by the noise level, one would never guess it.

As evening drew near, the day's festivities came to an end. On the news, the weather forecast showed a hard freeze warning. Sidney and Paul went out to the barn to put extra hay in the stalls. They returned with the cat and dog in tow. Apparently, Sidney had a weak moment and couldn't bear the thought of the newest members of the family spending a cold night in the barn. Eli and Grace were thrilled of course and made comfy beds for their new friends. All day, the children had thought of names for the pets. It was decided that the dog would be called Blue since she had one blue eye. The cat would carry the name of Rudolph or Rudy for short to remind them of Santa's great gift.

As the children drifted off to sleep, the house was quiet and still. A roaring fire blazed as Bridget and Paul sat on the couch and sipped a glass of wine.

"It's going to be a cold one tonight." Bridget commented as she pulled the blanket over her feet. "It's been a good Christmas, despite our setbacks. I say we toast to an even better Christmas next year."

Paul lifted his glass and added to the toast. "Here's to a better year for all of us. I know I'll find steady work, and we can get back on our feet. God will help us find our way. Here's to us and new beginnings."

Bridget raised her glass. She hated to ruin the moment, but somehow she knew better than to rely on God to help her with anything. She longed for the moment for him to prove her wrong. However, like every other Christmas Day for the past ten years, God remained silent. It was just as well because she wasn't ready to listen anyway.

Chapter 7
Icy Conditions

The two weeks of Christmas vacation came and went. A new year had begun, and Bridget was looking forward to the idea of being able to start fresh. As Bridget, Eli, and Grace rode to school on a cold January morning, they discussed ideas for Paul's approaching birthday. Bridget, however, knew that the best gift that he could receive was a full time job. There was still no news on when his company would begin construction again at the sugar refinery. Rumors had started in town that the Lyon Construction Company had been awarded a big contract to build an outlet mall near the interstate. It wasn't an industrial job typical for the company, but Lyon's was the best in the entire southern region of Louisiana. So, Paul was hopeful that for once, rumors could prove to be true.

On the ride home, Bridget and the children finalized plans for a surprise party for Paul. Since forty was the new twenty, Bridget decided to go with a roaring twenties theme. Uncle Sidney's attic was filled with old clothing, hats, and memorabilia from eras gone by. She knew that she could find props, so all she really needed was a few rolls of streamers, balloons, and a great cake from the local bakery. She had a few weeks to plan and send out invites, but sneaking around Paul, and keeping Grace from spilling the beans, were going to pose a problem. She only hoped that her plans would go off without a hitch.

January winters in Louisiana were always wet and harsh, sometimes unpredictable. It had been an unusually cold winter season with many days of freezing temperatures. Forecasts for the next few days were predicting a slight chance of snow and ice, which was a huge deal. Every kid in town was bursting with excitement for a chance to see snow. Grown-ups were buzzing in every shop and workplace as they carefully monitored the weather conditions.

School was closed for the next two days. Children and teachers rejoiced as the news was broadcast over the intercom by the principal. Local businesses were also planning on closing due to the possible icy road conditions. As Bridget drove by the supermarket, she noticed the parking lot was packed. Shoppers were stocking up in preparation for the next few days. Bridget smiled and laughed. She was glad that she had planned ahead and had bought groceries yesterday.

When they arrived home, Eli and Grace jumped out of the car to run out to the barn to check on the animals and fill Uncle Sidney in on the good news. Bridget hauled all of their book sacks and belongings into the house. She was just as thrilled as the children to be off for an extra-long weekend. She could spend the days finishing up invitations and catching up on her scrapbooking. Bridget turned on the coffee pot and scanned over the mail. Nothing but junk mail, so she brewed a cup of coffee for herself and Uncle Sidney. She put on her coat and walked toward the barn with coffee in hand. Sidney and the children were cleaning stalls and filling them with extra hay for the nights ahead. Grace insisted on bringing old blankets from the loft for the animals to snuggle. Rudy and Blue seemed unfazed by the ruckus. They knew that their beds inside would be most comfortable and warm.

As the evening hours arrived, the temperatures began dropping drastically. The children were glued to the windows, anxiously awaiting a glimpse of snow. Sidney and Paul watched the weather forecast every thirty minutes. Bridget was busy on the computer sorting through photographs to download into a digital scrapbook for the kids. Ann sat on the recliner crocheting a blanket. Ann was also part of the snow day sleepover, as Grace called it. Bridget's dad was working offshore again, so Sidney worried about her being home alone in the icy conditions, especially if the power went out. And, of course, Blue and Rudy slept soundly, nestled in blankets near the fireplace with not a care in the world.

By nine o'clock, Eli and Grace drifted off to sleep. Paul carried them upstairs to bed. Eli woke for a moment and told his dad to wake him and Grace up if it started to snow. Paul promised and tucked them into bed. From the looks of the current weather, if snow was to arrive, it would be in the early morning hours.

Paul joined Bridget at the kitchen table. Bridget sighed, "I do hope it snows tomorrow. I'm about as bad as Eli and Grace. I want to play in it too!"

Paul laughed, "If I see snow, do you want me to wake you up, too? Eli made me promise. I assume you want in on that?"

"Well, yeah! And for your information, it is going to snow. You'll see. I put in a special request for snow to Santa when he was here."

"Really? Well, you do know I'm in tight with St. Nick? If you fix me some hot chocolate and rub my feet, I could put in a good word for you!" Paul had a devilish grin across his face.

Bridget stood up and waved her hands about. "Oh, it's going to snow alright. You'll see. I hope it snows ten inches just to spite you! And it's going to snow without your so-called good words for Santa! Thanks for the offer, but I'll chance it." Bridget couldn't help but laugh at Paul's foolishness. Deep in her heart though, she really wished for snow.

About five o'clock the next morning, Bridget was awakened by a text message on her phone. Her sister, another snow freak, texted, "Good morning! You might want to look outside! It's snowing! Text me back in a bit!"

Bridget jumped out of bed with a thud. She ran to the window and threw back the curtains. Snow was slowly drifting through the air. She rushed to Paul's side of the bed and woke him up. "Looks like I was a good girl this year. Guess what Santa brought me this morning? Snow! Snow! Snow!" Bridget giddily jumped up and down in the bed.

Before Paul could get dressed, Bridget raced to the children's rooms. "Eli, Grace, get up and come see what I see!" The children rubbed their eyes and met Bridget at the window. It was still dark outside, but the porch lights were enough to allow them to see the white flakes steadily falling. Eli and Grace screamed with excitement and ran to Ann and Sidney's rooms to fill them in.

By five-thirty, everyone was bright-eyed and bushy tailed. Dressed in coats, hats, and gloves, Eli and Grace ran into the yard trying to catch snowflakes. Bridget soon joined them. Paul was taking pictures and videos of the rare Louisiana wintry event. Sidney and Ann looked on under the shelter of the porch and laughed as the children spun around in utter delight.

After a brief playtime, coats and gloves were thrown in the dryer as everyone came inside to warm up. Ann and Bridget started breakfast. Sidney watched the morning news and read the newspaper. Paul was posting a few pictures on Facebook and Instagram and checking through the email. Eli and Grace stayed glued to the windows until it was time for their favorite morning cartoons.

As the day went on, snow showers lingered. The ground was completely covered in a blanket of white. Eli and Grace had managed to build a small snowman on the courtyard. Paul initiated a snowball fight, and Bridget insisted on making snow angels in the yard. Even Blue and Rudy seemed to be enjoying themselves as they romped through the snow and chased after the children.

Shortly after noon, widespread power outages began to occur. The power lines just couldn't bear the weight of the accumulating ice and snow. Luckily, Sidney's fireplace and gas stove would keep them warm enough. By the light of hurricane lanterns, Paul and Eli played checkers. Grace contentedly played with her Barbie doll. Ann heated hot chocolate on the stove as she reminisced with Sidney about a few snowfalls during their youth. Bridget listened for a while, then grabbed her cell phone to check out the photos of the snow that all her family and friends had surely posted on Facebook.

As Bridget scanned though her news feed, a picture of her grandmother popped up without warning. She gasped and dropped the phone. Ann, sensing something was wrong, sat beside her. "Bridget, what's wrong? You look like you've seen a ghost!"

"I think I might have seen one. Look at this." She held the phone up for her mother to see the photo. "It just appeared out of nowhere. And this isn't the first time. What do you think it means?"

Ann took the phone and examined the photo. "I think it means she is watching over us, and she likes to let us know that she's thinking about us. Of course, you could go with your cousin Delia's theory. You've heard that she's been seeing her dead aunt again, haven't you? Apparently she has powers to talk to the dead. Who knew?"

Bridget raised her eyebrows in disbelief, "Oh brother. Don't get me started on that nonsense. I think Delia's blood sugar drops so low that she hallucinates! You know she's always on some fad diet. Either that or she's hitting the vodka again. I mean, I'm a little superstitious when it comes to things like that, but I sure in the heck don't need Gloria sitting on the foot of my bed each night either."

Bridget looked upward, "Maw-Maw Gloria…a photo is fine. I hear you loud and clear."

Ann said, "Well, I must admit, I'm not in the market for a haunting or visit from the dead either, but sometimes I do wonder what it would be like to be able to see her and talk to her again. I have so many questions. Oh, if only Heaven had visiting hours."

Bridget crossed her arms. "Not me, no way. I don't want to talk to anyone."

Ann pondered the statement. "You mean, that if God gave you the chance to talk to Noelle, you would refuse? You wouldn't want to know about her at all?"

Bridget's eyes filled with anger and tears. "Yes, I'd love to know about my child, but God took that from me. He took her ten years ago before I could even hold her!" All eyes in the room were fixed on Bridget as she let out ten years of anguish. Once she started ranting, Bridget just couldn't stop. Raw emotions poured out of her like rain from a storm cloud. "I'll never get to see her grow up. I'll never get to buy her a prom dress or a wedding gown. I'll never know her children. Why did God do this to me? Why would he finally after five years of trying to have a child, take her away from us? What did I do wrong? Why does God hate me so much? And how can all of you just go on everyday like nothing happened? How do you go to church and pray to someone who has ripped out your very soul?"

Paul walked over and cautiously approached her. "No, leave me alone please. I can't deal with your pity, your everything is going to be okay sermon. It's like you forgot about her. And I know what you're going to say. It's been ten years, get over it. Well, I can't. Not a day goes by that I don't long for our child. And yes, I'm selfish. We have two beautiful children, so I shouldn't complain. But she was mine! She was mine! God, why? I'll never in a million years understand why!"

Paul embraced her with all his strength. No words could ease her pain. No actions could make her forgive herself or God at this point. He knew this was a battle that she would have to fight alone, with his support and love in the background. Guilt overcame him as he realized that he had missed all the signs of Bridget's struggles with Noelle's death. He felt her pain as his own and wondered if perhaps he had forgotten and forgiven too easily. His faith was so strong that he never allowed himself to be suffocated by doubt. He had failed her in a spiritual way. He should have done more, gave of himself more. But it was too late for regrets.

As he laid beside her in bed that night, Paul prayed a silent prayer to God. "Lord, please help Bridget find her way back to you. Please set her free from the daily struggles that she inflicts upon herself. Lord, give her the will to live in the present. Love her Lord. She believes in you. She just doesn't remember how to love you and put her faith in you. Please, dear Lord, melt the ice in her soul. Amen."

The next morning, Bridget was awakened by Grace standing at her bedside with a plate of waffles. Eli came in behind her with a glass of orange juice and a wad of newspaper. Apparently, they had decided to serve her breakfast in bed.

"Mamma, we got you something to eat in bed!" Grace announced proudly. "Maw-Maw Ann let me help mix the waffles up."

"Yeah, and I poured your juice and got you the newspaper to read." Eli piped in with his contribution.

"Well, this looks delicious! Why all the special treatment this morning? Is it my birthday?" Bridget couldn't help but laugh at their efforts.

"No, Mamma. We know it's not your birthday, silly!" Eli giggled. "We just wanted you to feel better. We know you were sad yesterday. Are you going to be okay today?"

Bridget swallowed hard as a lump in her throat developed. Her outburst caused her children to fret. The last thing in the world that she wanted was for her son and daughter to worry. They had heard the story time and time again about the baby that was lost. Each December, Bridget put a heart on the calendar to mark Noelle's birthday. And each year when the children forgot its meaning, she reminded them about their special sister in Heaven.

She mustered a smile for them. "I feel just fine today. I'm sorry if I made you worry. Mommy just has to have a good cry every now and then about Noelle. I miss her very much. But, I promise, I am not sad anymore. Come give me some hugs for this wonderful breakfast."

They hugged each other tightly. Bridget invited them to sit in the bed with her for a while. They talked about the snow and how many snowmen they were going to build today. The newspaper had ample pictures of the snow covered areas around town, as well as a list of roads and businesses that were closed. Looking at the weather section, it was apparent that the snow would be around for at least another day before melting.

When Bridget finished her breakfast, Eli and Grace took the dishes downstairs. Bridget got dressed in sweatpants and her favorite LSU sweatshirt. She found a cozy pair of wool socks, then put on her slippers. As she brushed her hair into a ponytail, Bridget stared at her reflection in the mirror. Who was this stranger before her? How did she allow the last ten years of pain to consume her so? Something had to give. Bridget knew that she had to find a way to finally put closure to the past. She was not going to allow her children and her family to suffer. Somehow, she would find a way to let it go.

Apologies were first in order to Paul, her mother, and uncle for her behavior. As she entered the kitchen, Bridget poured herself a cup of coffee and sat down at the table with her family. She cleared her throat. "I'm sorry for what happened yesterday. I acted horribly. It's just…it's just that I have feelings that have been bottled up inside for ten years. And it's my own fault that I haven't talked to anyone about them before yesterday. For years, I've been hoping that some miracle would happen, and I could move on and let Noelle go. But it's apparent that I couldn't. I promise that I will try and accept what is in the past. I just need some time and understanding."

Ann walked over and hugged her daughter. "Honey, we didn't realize how much pain you were in after all this time. It hasn't been easy on any of us, but I suppose we all found ways to move on with life, and you didn't do the same. We should have been more attentive. If there's anything we can do, please promise you will ask us."

Bridget nodded tearfully. Paul took her hands in his across the table. "I loved our baby too. It's not that I've ever forgotten her. How could I forget my own child? I guess we all deal with grief differently. I had to keep going on with life as usual to survive, to cope. My faith was shaken for a while, but I realized that God must have had a purpose for our child. We may not know the reason or understand why, but we have to believe it was his will. I hope you can understand him one day and forgive him and forgive yourself. I love you, and I need you. Whatever it takes, we can get through this together. We can talk to Father John, a counselor, a friend, whoever you want. I just need my wife back beside me in church, loving the Lord, and walking with me eternally in Heaven."

"Okay, I'll try to figure out what I need to do to fix this hurt. I just need all of you to be patient. I love y'all, too." Bridget wiped the tears falling down her cheeks. Just then, the power came on. Everyone rejoiced. Bridget shook off the emotional overload and told the kids to get bundled up for a romp in the snow. She needed some fun and laughter. How her transformation was to come about, she hadn't a clue. But for once in ten years, Bridget was hopeful that change was on the horizon.

Chapter 8
BROKEN

In the passing weeks, Bridget did make an honest attempt to change her heart. She began attending mass again and had made herself talk to God again each morning on her ride to school. She had to admit that she felt better, but something still felt empty inside. Maybe God would find a way to fill in the gaps. She had tried to meet him halfway. Perhaps God would do the same.

Paul's birthday party was next on her plate. After weeks of planning and sneaking around, the party was a huge success. She was proud that Grace had not spilled the beans until an hour before the guests arrived, when she told Paul that he better get dressed up before his party. Bridget made him promise to act surprised. Everyone enjoyed dressing in twenties style. Paul looked so handsome in his gangster hat and suspenders. The ladies all wore flapper style dresses and feather headbands. The party was a riot! When Sidney and Ann showed everyone the Charleston and the Foxtrot, the room bursted with laughter and excitement. Bridget was having the best time. She even forgot her troubles for a few short hours.

The party was in full swing until about midnight. Guests reluctantly began their farewells. Bridget was wide awake and too wired to go to sleep, so she told Paul that she would clean up the party mess. Everyone else headed upstairs for the night. Soft music from Uncle Sidney's Victrola played in the quiet background. Bridget enjoyed the peaceful solitude. She got to work and scrubbed the kitchen until it shined. With arms full of trash bags, she headed outside to the garbage can. Blue followed behind her for one last outing.

She tossed the bags in and closed the lid. A pair of yellow eyes met hers! Bridget screamed and began sprinting across the wet lawn. Blue was barking wildly at the critter. Bridget quickly turned to call for Blue and suddenly lost her footing on a patch of wet mud. She could see herself falling backward as if in slow motion. She instinctively put her hands out to her sides to brace her fall. Crack! The moment that she heard the sound, Bridget knew that she had broken her arm. She squealed in pain and immediately felt nauseous and faint. It was the worst pain she had ever felt. Blue rushed to her side.

Bridget shakily told the dog, "Go get Paul. Go on. Go see Paul!"

The dog did as she was commanded. Blue ran upstairs and woke Paul up. The dog led Paul downstairs and outside to where Bridget lay in pain.

"Bridget! Are you okay? What happened?" Paul carefully picked her up and carried her inside. Bridget explained the ordeal. After cleaning mud off her hands and feet, Bridget changed her clothing to head for the emergency room.

The ER was relatively quiet at two o'clock in the morning. Paul checked in and filled out paperwork as Bridget sat impatiently waiting to see the doctor. She hated hospitals. The whole place made her uncomfortable. How her sister worked in the hospital setting was beyond Bridget's comprehension. An ambulance pulled under the carport, which made Bridget all the more uneasy. And, of course, it meant that she would have to wait a while longer to be seen.

Paramedics rolled the patient down the hall. A familiar voice could be heard as they filled the nurses in on vital signs. Bridget knew that voice. She leaned over to look down the hallway. It was a former student, Joseph. They made eye contact, and Joe waved and came toward her.

"Hey Mrs. Bridget. What are you doing in the ER?" He hugged her and stood beside her.

"Joe, it's so good to see you! I'm afraid I probably broke my arm. I slipped outside in the yard running from a critter by our garbage can. Scared me half to death!"

Just then, the admitting clerk called Paul to her desk to go over paperwork and insurance. Bridget asked Joe to sit for a moment. "Wow! It's been years, hasn't it? I still remember you as that cute little rascal in my second grade class. How have you been?"

"Oh, I'm alright. I'm sure you heard that I got expelled last year." Bridget nodded. "It was stupid really. Not my best moment for sure. But you'd be proud of me. I did get my GED. I'm training to be a paramedic, so hopefully that will work out now that I'm on my own and all."

Bridget had heard that Joe's mother had tossed him to the wind again, just as she always had when he was a child. His mother was a drug addict. When she was clean, life was good for Joe. But when she would revisit the old habit, Joe was always sent to live at his grandparents' house. His dad was in and out of jail for various misdemeanors, so poor Joe grew up with no stability, just a broken, godless home. Bridget always worried about students like Joe. What chance did kids like him have in this world? However, she was more than thrilled to see that Joe might just make something of his life.

"Well, Joe, I am proud of you for finishing school. I'm sure that wasn't easy, but at least you had the good sense to know how important a diploma is to your future. I think you are going to make a fine paramedic, too. Just stick with whatever you choose to do in life and don't give up. If you can take care of yourself and become a responsible, independent young man, then the possibilities are endless. Just be sure to choose your friends wisely. Don't repeat history."

Joe looked a bit taken back. "Thanks Mrs. Bridget. You know you're the only person who thinks I can actually be successful, besides my grandparents, of course. All my friends think I'm nuts to want to work all the time. Most have them have quit school and sit around the house all day. As time goes by, I'm beginning to see things a lot differently. Who knows, maybe I'm finally growing up!"

"As I said, watch the company you keep. You are so smart and so capable. Don't let a split second lack of judgment ruin your life. Maybe you need new friends. I know that I wouldn't let anyone tell me not to pursue my dreams. I'm sure you'll find some better acquaintances at work. You could always try church to meet new people. Just promise me that you will work hard and stay out of trouble."

Joe smiled and stood to get back to work. "I promise I'll do my best. Thanks for always believing in me. Even though I know I drove you crazy, you were one of my favorite teachers. You never cut me any slack. Maybe I'll take you up on the church thing one day. The girls I've been meeting lately are lousy."

Bridget laughed as she hugged him goodbye. Paul returned with a diet coke in hand. He always knew what she needed. A few minutes later, Bridget was checked into a room. A tech came in with a mobile X-ray machine and scanned her arm. The nurse followed in behind her and took Bridget's vital signs and asked about the fall. Shortly after she got comfortable on the table, the ER doctor appeared with the news that the arm was indeed broken. He put a splint on the arm and prescribed pain medication for a few days. Bridget would have to see an orthopedic doctor for further X-rays and a cast once the swelling went down.

Paul and Bridget returned home in the wee hours of the morning. Bridget was exhausted. She tossed and turned for a while, thinking about Joe and their conversation. She was touched by Joe's determination to make something of himself. Until tonight, she had no idea that her influence as a teacher had been so profound. It had been nine years since Joe had graced her classroom, but apparently her lessons were lasting. She had made a difference in his life, and for that she was most grateful. Before falling asleep, Bridget said a prayer for Joe. She asked God to protect him and guide his decisions. Joe deserved a good life.

Chapter 9

EVELYN

Mid-February brought about Mardi Gras and a few days off of school. Bridget was grateful for the down time. Her broken arm proved to be an exhausting, daily challenge, but luckily the cast was to come off in a week. Eli and Grace were excited about the parades and talked about it non-stop. Beads, doubloons, and trinkets would be scattered from one end of the house to the other for weeks on end.

The phone rang. Paul was on his way home from the construction site at the new outlet mall. God had answered his prayer for a steady job again. He was on his way to the bakery and needed to ask Grace about which flavor king cake to bring home. It was Grace's turn to choose. Bridget handed her the phone. Grace asked for a strawberry and cream cheese filled king cake.

Twenty minutes later, Paul was pulling into the driveway with the king cake in hand. Bridget cut a small piece for Eli and Grace and sent them off to watch their favorite afternoon TV show. Bridget fixed Paul an afternoon cup of coffee. As they sat at the table, Paul seemed a bit worried.

"Penny for your thoughts, Paul. Something on your mind?" Bridget sipped her coffee, waiting for his reply.

"I saw Evelyn's aunt in the bakery just now. She told me that Evelyn was admitted to the hospital earlier. Apparently, she passed out at work. She told me that the doctors were running some tests."

Bridget immediately grabbed her phone to text Evelyn's husband, Jack. "Oh my goodness! I need to see what's going on. She seemed a little off during your birthday party, but I chalked it up to a long day at work. I was supposed to call her this weekend to see if they were going to catch the Mardi Gras parade with us as usual. I hope she's okay."

Bridget typed as fast as her fingers would allow. She anxiously awaited a response. Paul rubbed her shoulders in comfort. "I'm sure she's fine. They are just being extra cautious."

Moments later, Evelyn's husband replied that she was still in the hospital, awaiting more tests and results from an MRI. It sounded fairly serious. As she read the text aloud to Paul, he urged her to go to the hospital to be with Evelyn. He would fix supper for the children. She kissed him on her way out and promised to keep him updated.

As Bridget drove to the hospital, an uneasy feeling in the pit of her stomach arose. Something was terribly wrong with her friend. She prayed to God aloud, asking him for good news. She begged him to watch over Evelyn. It was the first time she had a sincere, friendly conversation with him in quite a while. She only hoped that he was listening.

Bridget practically sprinted through the hospital parking lot. At the nurse's station, she inquired about Evelyn and was directed to a room in the ER. As she made her way to Evelyn's room, she passed her sister in the hall. Bridget forgot that it was her regular shift today. "Bridget, what are you doing here? Everything okay with Paul and the kids?"

"Elizabeth, I'm glad to see you. I'm here for Evelyn. She had a fainting episode at work and is here for tests. She had an MRI earlier. It sounds serious. Have you heard anything about her case?"

"No, not yet. I just got here about ten minutes ago, so I haven't had a chance to check the board and charts. I'll look into it and stop by her room in a bit. Bridget, don't panic. Tests don't always mean it's something serious. Doctors just like to be thorough."

Bridget was comforted by Elizabeth's thoughts. Perhaps she was overreacting. She knocked on the door and walked into Evelyn's room all smiles, putting on a brave face. "Hello my BFF, how are you?" Bridget walked over to the bedside and gave her a hug.

Evelyn shrugged and laughed, "Oh, you know some of us will do anything to get out of going back to work! You know I live for holidays and sick days."

Bridget sat on the edge of the bed and teased Jack. "What's the matter, she isn't getting enough attention at home?" They all snickered and commented on her flair for the dramatic. An hour passed, and the three of them made small talk about the weather, Mardi Gras, their children, work, and so on. Passing time was so hard.

A knock on the door startled them. Bridget and Jack stood as the doctor walked in with a chart in his hand. Evelyn asked if the tests showed anything beyond exhaustion from too many long hours at work. The doctor sat at Evelyn's bedside with a stern look. Bridget thought that she would throw up. Her heart was beating so fast, she felt as though she was having a panic attack. The news was not good, and she knew it.

The doctor sighed heavily and began to explain to Evelyn that her tests indicated that she had a tumor that could be cancerous. It was confined to her ovaries from what her scans showed; however, they wouldn't know anything definite until they operated to remove the tumor and ovaries.

Bridget held back tears and bit her lip so hard that it bled. Evelyn just sat there in silence. For a moment, her world stopped turning. Jack began asking questions about the surgery and the treatment. If it was cancer, then he needed to know what Evelyn would be facing. Bridget listened attentively in case Jack couldn't take it all in. She knew from her experience with her grandmother that it would all be a blur for them. Someone with a level head would have to listen and confirm what was happening next. Why she was the chosen messenger was beyond her comprehension.

When the doctor left, Bridget held Evelyn's hand and comforted her as best she could. What does one say in such a situation? Bridget had not a clue. She left the room to give Evelyn and Jack a moment alone to absorb the reality of it all. Surgery was scheduled for Monday morning. How would her friend survive the weekend not knowing her fate?

Bridget went to the end of the hall and called Paul. Crying, she told him of Evelyn's diagnosis. Paul insisted on coming to the hospital, but Bridget refused. She didn't want the kids to worry. Evelyn's children would have to be told…oh, the thought raced through her mind like wildfire. Bridget had to get herself together in a hurry. She would not let her friend see her upset. Bridget had to be positive and upbeat for her friend. She went to the vending machine and bought a diet coke and Evelyn's favorite candy bar. Knowing full and well Evelyn would refuse both, Bridget just couldn't think of anything else to do to be helpful.

Bridget ran into Elizabeth in the hall. Elizabeth had read the test results on Evelyn's chart. She comforted her sister and reassured her that she would be at the hospital all night, so she promised to check in on Evelyn and report any changes. Bridget thanked her and headed back to Evelyn's room. The mood in the room was somber. Evelyn told Bridget that Jack had called her parents and told them the news. They were on their way. Bridget offered her the diet coke and candy bar and lay them on the tray near the bed. Bridget knew that Evelyn would need private time with her family to soak in the news. She bid her friend goodnight and promised to visit tomorrow. Jack walked her to the door. She hugged him and told him that she would text him before she visited to make sure Evelyn was up for it. She offered to keep the children or help in any way. Jack thanked her for the offer. His only request was for her to pray.

Bridget drove home and pondered Jacks request. Pray. Pray? Did he not realize that God didn't seem to listen to Bridget's prayers? It was as if her every request fell upon deaf ears, or so she thought. Why would God listen now? Bridget was trying to forgive God, but was he ready to forgive her and listen to her prayers? She only hoped that her prayers, along with so many others, would reach God's ears. Her friend's life may very well depend upon it.

Chapter 10
Never Let Go

Sunshine beamed through the bedroom window as Bridget tossed and turned. It was Saturday morning, which meant the kids would be sleeping late. Bridget normally would have slept in as well, but Evelyn's condition weighed heavily on her mind. At eight o'clock, Bridget could stand it no longer. She got up, washed her face, and went downstairs to fix a nice, big breakfast for Paul and the kids. Uncle Sidney already had the coffee hot and ready. Bridget fixed herself a cup and glanced out the window to see her uncle pruning his prize rose bushes for spring.

She gathered the ingredients for French toast and began cooking. She checked her phone to see if she had missed any calls or texts from Jack or her sister…nothing. Bridget would wait and venture to the hospital around lunch time. She would have to pretend all was well for now in front of the kids. They would know soon enough. Grace and Evelyn's daughter, Kate, were the best of friends, too. Bridget recalled how she and Evelyn first met. Grace and Kate were in the same dance class. Bridget and Evelyn would wait for the girls in the waiting room during class. One friendly conversation led to another. It was as though Evelyn and Bridget were kindred spirits. They had so much in common. It was easy for the two of them to become so close, so fast.

When the girls quit dance to move on to other interests, Evelyn and Bridget remained in contact. They would meet for lunch, so the girls could play and visit. Birthdays, holidays, and even some vacations were spent together. Their friendship developed into a sisterhood. Despite the fact that Bridget had only known Evelyn for five years, it was though they had known each other for a lifetime. Bridget couldn't bear the thought of losing her, not now, not ever.

After Paul and the kids rolled out of bed and were fed French toast, Bridget hurried upstairs to get ready. She threw on her favorite T-shirt and yoga pants and put her hair up in a ponytail. A quick makeup job to hide her imperfections, and Bridget was ready to go. She texted Jack to check on Evelyn's mood to see if she was ready for company. Minutes later, Jack texted that company would be most appreciated. Bridget put a few leftover pieces of French toast in a container for Evelyn. She loved Bridget's French toast. Maybe she would eat something.

Bridget kissed Eli and Grace goodbye. She lied and told them that a few of her friends were meeting for lunch and shopping. She had to lie for now, for there were no other options. Paul followed Bridget to the car and asked her to tell Evelyn that he was thinking about her.

The downtown area was festively decorated in purple, green, and gold for Mardi Gras and the big parade in town on Sunday. The kids chatted constantly this morning about the parade. It was one of the highlights of the year for the locals. Even though there was no reason to celebrate this year, Bridget knew that there was no way that she could disappoint the kids and not attend the parade. Suddenly, the Coffee House sign caught her attention. She pulled into a parking spot in front of the store. She figured Jack would appreciate a decent cup of coffee. Bridget ordered three coffees to go. Coffee would go great with the French toast. How could Evelyn resist two of her favorite things?

Bridget arrived at the hospital ten minutes later. She took a deep breath and mumbled a quick prayer for strength before entering the room. With a smile, Bridget packed the goodies into the room. "Hello my friend. How are you feeling today? I've brought some treats for us to share. I hope you're in the mood for my famous French toast and some coffee from the Coffee House."

Jack commented on how good it smelled and took his coffee and fixed it to his liking. Evelyn handed him her cup and told him to fix hers as well. Bridget was encouraged. Jack dove into the French toast next and commented on how lousy the cafeteria food was this morning. Evelyn took a small piece as well. She picked at it mostly, but at least she had made the effort.

Bridget asked Jack if he had been home yet and if he had told the children. Both answers were no. Bridget told Jack that she was going to stay for the afternoon. She encouraged him to go home and get a good shower, some rest, and tend to the children. He reluctantly agreed, but only after Evelyn insisted that she was in good hands. When the two friends were alone, Bridget asked,

"Evelyn, how long have you been feeling under the weather? I noticed at Paul's birthday party that you looked tired. I thought it was work. I'm sorry I didn't ask sooner. Maybe if I had…"

"Maybe if you had, I wouldn't be here? That's horse pucky! I started feeling bad around Thanksgiving. I started hurting in my abdominal area. I had seen my doctor for an annual visit back in July. We discussed some pre-menopause symptoms that I was experiencing. I just thought that the cramps and pain were part of going through the change. I called for a prescription for cramps. It helped a bit. The doctor told me to call back after the holidays if the pain persisted. But, you know how it is as a mother. We are too busy tending to everyone else to take care of ourselves. But I will have you know before you fuss me that I did have an appointment scheduled at the end of this month. Looks like it's too little too late."

Bridget sat next to her friend. "It's never too late to take care of yourself. And don't blame yourself. I probably would have done the same exact thing. I mean when you don't know what's normal or not normal with your body, then you tend to just put it off as something else. And gosh knows that the internet is no help at all. You type in a symptom and you automatically have some rare disease! And let's face it, once you are over forty, your whole body goes to pot! Sometimes I think doctors just pacify women with pills and pamphlets to get us out of the office. But let a man whine about a hang nail, and he'd be admitted in a heartbeat!"

Evelyn started laughing. "Preach on Sista Bridget! Oh, you are the best medicine for me. You always make me laugh. But try not to worry. It's all in God's hands now. I have to believe that he will take care of me in good times and bad times. Just pray for me and my family. It's going to be so hard telling Kate and Kade about the possibility of cancer." Tears filled her eyes as she pondered her children's reaction to the news.

Bridget told Evelyn that she would look after the children and take them to the parade to keep their spirits up. Kate and Kade could stay with them as long as necessary. School was out anyway until Thursday for the Mardi Gras holiday. Eli and Grace could keep their minds off their troubles. Evelyn agreed to the arrangement for the children's sake. Her recuperation time in the hospital would at least be a few days. She knew that she would need Jack and her parents' help for the first few days after she went home.

Bridget's afternoon with Evelyn ended, as Jack returned with Kate and Kade. She walked slowly back to the car. She climbed in, turned on the engine, and buckled her seatbelt. She laid her head on the steering wheel and cried. Her heart was breaking for Evelyn and for what she was about to tell her children. Their lives would never be the same. How was that fair? Why did good people suffer?

The clouds of doubt once again shadowed Bridget's soul. First Noelle, now Evelyn. She screamed, "What else do you want from me God? Haven't you taken enough from me? Why? God, please answer me! Why? I'm trying to understand. I'm trying to let the past go. Is this a test of my faith? Please don't take her away from me, too. Please let her stay."

Bridget wiped her tears away and left the hospital. She drove home in a daze. Paul met her outside and comforted her. She told him about keeping Kate and Kade for the holiday as Evelyn recovered from surgery. Before their arrival, Eli and Grace had to be told and coached on how to handle the situation. Paul insisted on telling the children for her. He could be calm and reassuring. Bridget would be an emotional basket case. Eli and Grace were on the courtyard playing with Blue and Rudy. Paul sat them down and told them about Evelyn's condition. Bridget looked on from a distance. She could hear them asking Paul questions about cancer and how someone could get it, and so on. Bridget fought back tears. Her children were being brave and handling the news better than expected.

Jack arrived with Kate and Kade later that same evening. Bridget reassured Jack that the kids would be fine and would be by after the parade to visit Evelyn. Eli and Grace took them upstairs to their home away from home. In no time, laughter and ruckus could be heard. Jack looked relieved that the kids would have a few days of fun before reality hit.

Early the next morning, the kids were wide awake and bouncing off the walls with excitement. The annual Mardi Gras parade was going to be underway at noon. Usually, Bridget looked forward to the event, but this year was different. Evelyn would not be there beside her dancing and fighting over silly beads. Bridget recalled previous years of fun. She couldn't help but smile as she thought about the good times. In that moment, Bridget vowed that there would be many more years of parades and other events with her friend. She wouldn't have it any other way.

The parade went on as usual with floats, marching bands, and street performers. The children caught beads, trinkets, stuffed animals, and candy. Bags filled with parade loot were hauled back to the car. Later that evening, Paul and Bridget took the kids for pizza and a visit with Evelyn. The children had selected a few of their prize throws from the parade to show Evelyn.

As the children entered the room, they pretended to be in the parade. Evelyn laughed and clapped and hollered for them to throw her something good. It was wonderful to see her in such joyful spirits, knowing surgery awaited her come morning. The kids did a show and tell, and told a detailed account of the parade. They went around the room and hung beads on door knobs and the blinds so that Evelyn could celebrate Mardi Gras, too. After the room had been properly decorated, Jack and Paul took them to the cafeteria for dessert. It was the perfect opportunity for Bridget to spend time with Evelyn and put her mind at ease.

"So, are you ready for tomorrow?" Bridget nervously asked.

"Amazingly, I am. I don't know how to explain it, but I have a sense of calmness and peace. I feel like God is watching over me. Now, don't get me wrong, I am still worried. But I know it's in God's hands. Whatever will be, will be. It's out of my control."

"You are a brave woman. A lot of people are praying for you and for good news. And don't fret over the kids. They are having a blast at my house, as you can tell. The only thing you need to worry about is getting through surgery tomorrow and getting better. You know I'm here for you. I'll be here bright and early to wish you luck."

Evelyn and Bridget held hands tightly. They spent a few moments chatting and joking, just as they always had every time they were together. Bridget silently prayed for God to never let their friendship end. In her private thoughts, she begged him to be merciful. She never wanted to let Evelyn go.

Chapter 11

Going to the Chapel

At six o'clock in the morning, the waiting room was filled with Evelyn's family and friends from work and church. As Evelyn's surgery began, Father John gathered the crowd and said a prayer for healing and recovery. Well-wishers came and went as the morning lingered. Bridget had to walk around. The waiting was killing her. She went outside to give Uncle Sidney a quick call to check on the kids. Evelyn had requested that Kate and Kade not spend their day at the hospital.

Bridget aimlessly roamed the hallways, trying to find any distraction to keep her mind busy. The smell of cafeteria food made her nauseous, so she kept walking. The gift shop caught her eye, so she ventured inside. Bridget half-heartedly browsed through the get well cards and novelty items. A bouquet of pink roses in the cooler reminded her of Evelyn. Pink roses were her absolute favorite. Bridget asked the florist on duty about plants and flowers available for same day delivery. She was tempted to order the roses, but perhaps that was a surprise more appropriate from Jack and the kids. She chose a beautiful peace lily instead and requested a pink bow and pink balloon to go along with it. The florist assured her that it would be delivered later in the afternoon.

On her way back to the waiting room, Bridget came upon the hospital chapel. She stopped in her stride and debated whether or not to go inside. As luck would have it, an older gentleman exited and held the door open for Bridget as a courtesy. She had no choice now. She thought to herself, "I'm going Lord, I'm going." She lit a candle for her friend and sat in the pew. She took a deep breath and spent a few tender moments begging God for mercy and compassion. She asked for understanding. She asked for God to hear her and give her the answers to make sense of Evelyn's condition. She sat a while longer, quietly waiting for his response.

Bridget looked down at her watch. She had been gone thirty minutes. She checked her cell phone for any missed calls or messages. It was probably time to make her way back to the waiting room to check on any updates. As she walked down the aisle, Bridget saw a familiar face. His eyes met hers as he stood to greet her. It was Joe.

"Joe, what a surprise. It's nice to see you again. What are you doing here?"

Joe sat back down and Bridget sat beside him. "My grandfather had a heart attack last night. He's undergoing a bypass this morning. I didn't know what else to do for my grandmother, so I figured maybe if I sat in here a while to think, to try to pray, it might help. Thing is Mrs. Bridget, I don't know how to pray. My parents never were church going people or believed in much of anything. My grandparents would take me to church sometimes and send me to vacation bible school, but beyond that, I don't have a relationship with God. I don't know if I believe he exists, but I'd like to learn more. How can I start? Can you help me and teach me how to pray?"

Bridget was taken back by his request. Was this a challenge that God had sent her way? How could she answer Joe? She wasn't all that close to God either. And she certainly wasn't an expert on prayer or church. However, as the same good teacher who guided him in second grade, Bridget knew Joe needed her help.

"Well, Joe, I'm no expert on God or church or prayer. And I do have to admit that my own relationship with God has not always been perfect. But I am trying to change my ways and get back to his good graces. To answer your question, first of all, if you want to learn more about God and the bible, then you can attend classes down at St. Joseph's. A lot of adults who are in your same predicament find it very helpful. If you aren't ready for that step yet, then just attend mass. Father John is an excellent priest and public speaker. He puts the bible into terms that anyone can understand. He's positive and puts the Lord's teachings in modern day terms. Now don't get me wrong, he doesn't sugar coat how you should live your life as a Christian, but it helps that he isn't all fire and brimstone."

"My grandmother really speaks highly of Father John. She helps clean the church with other ladies every few weeks and helps decorate for the holidays. She tries to get me to go to church all the time. I guess I'm just a bit nervous. Maybe I'll give it a try."

"Well, if St. Joseph's isn't the right fit, there are plenty of good churches in the area of different faiths. I've heard wonderful things about them as well. You're just going to have to find a church where you feel comfortable."

"Thanks. I'll look into it. Now, what about prayer? I know a few prayers. Is that what you say when you pray, or do you say something else special?"

"You can say certain prayers if that's what you feel comfortable doing. There are books of prayers you can buy at the local bookstore, or you can borrow a book from the church. Honestly though, I think just talking to God and sharing your needs works best for me. It's not hard. You just talk."

Joe thought for a second. "Hmm…like talking on the phone to a friend, right?" Bridget nodded. Joe seemed relieved. Bridget looked at her watch again. She really had to get back to check on Evelyn. Joe stopped her, "You never said why you were here at the hospital. Are your kids okay?"

"My friend is having surgery to remove a tumor. I'm praying that she'll be alright and that it isn't cancer. Thanks for asking. Tell your grandmother that I said hello. Hope your grandfather has a good recovery."

"Thanks. Now that I know how to talk to God, I'll be sure to ask him to look after your friend. You know what Mrs. Bridget, you still got it! Here I am, eighteen years old and still learning lessons from my second grade teacher. Funny, isn't it?" Bridget laughed. She hugged him goodbye. As she walked the hallways, a smile slid across her face. Joe was a good kid. And maybe, just maybe he had taught her something as well.

Back in the waiting room, Jack and Evelyn's parents, along with a few other friends and family, waited impatiently for news. Four hours later, the doctor emerged. The family gathered around to hear the prognosis. Evelyn's surgery had no complications. The ovaries had been removed. However, the tumor was cancerous and had spread to lymph nodes. The doctor's tone was grim. By his best medical opinion, the cancer was stage three at the very least. Evelyn's mother grasped her chest and had to sit. The doctor, sensing the mood of the room, also reassured the family that treatment was certainly an option and could begin in a few weeks. He gave a few statistics about survival rates and the success of chemotherapy and new experimental treatments. He had no plans of giving up on Evelyn. Jack thanked him and followed a nurse to Evelyn's recovery room.

The world spun in slow motion as Bridget took the news to heart. Her friend was in serious trouble. Evelyn would need her now more than ever. How could Bridget be strong for her friend? She was so weak in so many ways…weak in her faith, weak in her emotions, weak in her understanding. Evelyn was always the stronger one. She was the leader, the take charge kind of girl. She could have handled this so gracefully.

Bridget could stand it no longer. She ran out of the waiting room and to the parking lot. She had to go home to her children. She had to see Paul and tell him this in person. She cried as she drove to the construction site. She had to tell Paul now, or she would go crazy. Paul was on lunch break, so he spotted Bridget as she arrived. By one look at her, Paul knew the news was not good. Bridget ran to his embrace and buried her head into his chest. He comforted her the best he knew how. On his way home, he would stop and buy Bridget's favorite ice cream and some flowers to cheer her spirits. It was little to ease her pain, but he had to try.

Bridget drove home sobbing. As she turned down the highway that led home, she told herself to get a grip for Kate and Kade's sake. They didn't need to see her fall apart. *She* had to be the strong one now.

Chapter 12

Meet Mae

Bridget had many people whom she considered friends. Most were teachers at her school or moms of her children's friends. She was well respected by her peers and was always willing to lend a helping hand to anyone who asked. Bridget knew no strangers. She would carry on a conversation with whomever she came in contact. Despite her outward friendliness, Bridget had only two people in the world whom she trusted with her deepest secrets and her heart. Her friendship was guarded, but once you made the cut, you were her friend for an eternity.

Evelyn, of course, was one in her inner circle. The other chosen sister in Bridget's sisterhood was Mae. She had met Mae the first year she started teaching. Mae had been a tremendous help and aided in Bridget's survival of her first year. Mae was a few years older than Bridget, but the two hit it off immediately. They shared the same teaching philosophy and were teamed together on many school committees. A bond formed between them, and the rest was history.

Ten years ago, Mae had been there for Bridget during the loss of Noelle. Mae helped her cope and made sure she kept Bridget busy. Many Saturdays were spent at the Coffee House, the bookstore, or antiquing. Bridget was thankful for the distraction. Now, Bridget needed Mae again. She was out of town for the Mardi Gras holiday. Bridget didn't want to disturb her vacation with Evelyn's news. Mae would return on Wednesday, and not a moment too soon for Bridget.

Bridget recalled the day that she introduced Evelyn and Mae to one another. She hoped that they would hit it off as well so that the three of them could shop, do lunch, and let the kids play together without Bridget's time being divided. She loved each friend equally. But each represented something different in her life. Mae was the stable, calming force in Bridget's world. Mae could always be depended upon in a time of need and could bring Bridget back down to Earth. Evelyn was the feisty, fun loving side of Bridget's personality. Evelyn was continuously on the lookout for the next big adventure. They had cruised to the Caribbean, zip lined in the mountains, rode horses on the beach, and so on. Evelyn pushed Bridget to try new things and enjoy life. Mae and Evelyn did hit it off and became friends as well, not to the extent that Bridget loved them, but it was okay. Bridget had room for both of them in her world.

Bridget sat on the courtyard and watched the children play. Jack had arrived and told the children limited information on the seriousness of Evelyn's condition. They knew their mother would have treatments that might make her sick and lose her hair, but it stopped there. Death was never a word mentioned. Evelyn preferred it that way for the time being. She wanted her children to lead a normal life as long as possible. Bridget wondered how she would've handled the situation.

Bridget offered Jack another cup of coffee and an invitation to stay for supper. She knew that he hadn't eaten a decent meal in days. He accepted and spent the evening with the children, trying to put on a brave face. Bridget would have to do the same come morning. She knew that she had to face Evelyn. She opted not to return to the hospital after the surgery. She felt as though her family needed that time, and Bridget needed to regroup before seeing her friend.

She had spent the afternoon doing what she had always done when she was worrisome. Bridget cleaned until the house was spotless. Then, she cooked a meal to feed an army. Bridget had to feel useful. She packed Jack and Evelyn doggie bags for the freezer. Evelyn would appreciate not having to cook for a while. Before Jack left, she asked to borrow a house key so the children could get a few more things. Bridget would scrub Evelyn's house from top to bottom tomorrow. This would keep her at ease until Mae returned the next day.

Bridget tossed and turned all night, unable to sleep soundly. Her mind raced with things that she could say to comfort Evelyn. She thought about Kate and Kade and if keeping the whole truth about the grim nature of her prognosis from them was wise. She also thought about the tons of errands to run in town. The day wasn't going to be long enough to accomplish her to do list. As Paul's alarm clock went off at five o'clock, Bridget was still wide awake. She got up and made coffee and a quick breakfast for him before he headed to work. The early quiet hours minus the distraction of children proved to be productive. Bridget paid bills online, checked her email, polished her toenails, unloaded the dishwasher, and put red beans to soak in the crock pot for supper. She did a half day's work in three short hours.

After breakfast, Bridget made the children get dressed for the hospital. By ten o'clock, they had parked the car and were heading inside to visit Evelyn. Her room was cheerily filled with flowers, plants, and balloons from family and friends. It was nice to see that so many people regarded Evelyn so highly. As soon as she saw Kate and Kade, Evelyn held her arms open wide for a hug. Eli and Grace were next to give hugs and hellos. Then, the four of them sat on the couch and dove into a video game. So much for worrying about their reaction to seeing Evelyn. Bridget held back tears as she bent down to hug her friend. She smiled weakly and quickly commented on the beautiful arrangements from well-wishers. Bridget asked if there was anything she wanted or needed. Evelyn declined and told Bridget to just sit and visit for a while. Jack had to meet with the doctor to arrange a treatment schedule and fill out paperwork for insurance purposes. He would be gone a while, so Evelyn needed the company.

Not knowing what to say, Bridget talked about the cold weather moving in, the new goat Uncle Sidney had purchased, the horrible lines at the grocery store, whatever came to mind. She knew she was rambling, but she couldn't help it. Her nerves were on edge. Evelyn must have sensed it. "Geez, Bridget, get a grip! Slow down sista! I am not going anywhere soon. I got time ya know." She squeezed Bridget's hand. "It's okay. I'm going to fight this til there's no fight left in me. You don't have to pretend around me. I know you're afraid. I am, too. But we don't know what the future holds. When it's our time to go, there's nothing any of us can do about it. We just have to accept it."

Bridget wiped away tears. "I am scared and selfish. I don't want to lose you. We have so many more adventures to plan. It's just not fair. I, for the life of me, will never understand God's decisions. Just tell me what you want me to do, and I'll do it."

Evelyn sighed, "Honey, life isn't fair. And none of us are able to understand life, sickness, or death from God's perspective. I suppose if we could, then there would be no reason to have faith. Now, don't get me wrong, I'm angry. I wonder why me and not someone else. But I'll go crazy thinking that way. I just have to believe that there's a plan, and I'm part of that plan."

"Evelyn, you are way too gracious and calm. I'd be cursing and mad at the world. There's no way I could sit here and see the silver lining. Part of a plan, my foot! How do you do it? How can you sit here and be so faithful?" Bridget folded her arms in disgust.

"I can't explain it. Remember I told you about a sense of peace and calmness that I felt? Well, that feeling is stronger now than before my surgery. It's like God is showering me with his love and strength. Now, I'd never tell another soul this, including Jack, but something happened to me during my surgery." Bridget unfolded her arms and lowered her guard. "I was whisked away to the most beautiful garden. The garden had trees and meadows of wildflowers, waterfalls, and an ocean of the most majestic shade of turquoise. Animals of all kinds roamed the gardens, unafraid of the people there. It was so serene, so joyful."

Bridget was skeptical, of course. "I think you might have imagined the experience. I mean, I don't think you had a life after death experience, considering you never came close to death during the operation. Maybe it was the anesthesia messing with your mind. I think dying was on your mind, so your thoughts drifted in that direction."

Evelyn shook her head in disagreement, "No, it wasn't a dream. I'm telling you that I was there. It was too real."

Bridget, still not convinced, decided to play devil's advocate. "Well, did you see anyone you knew while you were in this magical garden?"

Evelyn explained, "Not this time, but the angel assigned to me said that on my next visit I would be reunited with familiar faces." Bridget listened and let Evelyn go on about her so-called experience. Evelyn went on to say that the angel was a bright light with no real shape. She was told that she would be able to see things more clearly as her visits continued. This angel of mercy, as she described, seemed to be a comfort. Bridget just let it go and decided not to question it. If it made Evelyn feel encouraged, then what was the harm?

Bridget changed the subject and began telling her about Mae's vacation to Boston with her daughters. They were visiting family, and no doubt enjoying a change of scenery. It had been a year since

Mae's bitter divorce. She had been so strong through it all for her daughters. She deserved happiness after the hell her husband had put her through. Bridget, not wanting to dampen their first vacation alone, told Evelyn that she had kept Mae in the dark about the cancer. Mae would arrive home soon. Bridget would bear the news.

Jack returned with the doctor. Dr. Monroe explained the chemotherapy schedule for twice a week and possible side effects. He recommended medications to help her deal with nausea, as well as natural remedies to ease the discomfort of treatments. Jack was given a list of cancer specialists and hospitals in other states. However, Dr. Monroe was one of the best cancer doctors in the state, and everyone knew his reputation well. It was up to Evelyn to decide where her treatment would take place. Bridget knew that her friend needed time to think, so she took the hint and left to run errands and get the kids some ice cream.

Uncle Sidney was out by the barn with the new goat. The kids jumped out of the car and ran squealing with delight at the sight of it. Supper was in the slow cooker and the house was immaculate. Bridget decided to drive to Evelyn's to pick up a few extra outfits for Kate and Kade. The house was in disarray. Bridget knew what she had to do. She immediately found cleaning supplies and scrubbed, vacuumed, mopped, dusted, and did a few loads of laundry. There was no way her friend would come home to a dirty house, for that was the last thing she needed to worry over. She took extra care in Evelyn's bedroom. Fresh sheets, fluffed pillows, aroma therapy candles, and a vase of roses from her own garden were in place for her arrival. Evelyn would come home tomorrow evening to a relaxing retreat.

Bridget looked at her phone for the time. She had missed a text message from Mae. She had sent a photo from Boston and reminded Bridget of her return flight arrival in New Orleans. Mae told her how much fun they were having, but she was ready to come home and catch up with Bridget over coffee. A wave of panic came over her. How would she tell Mae without falling apart? Mae, certainly, could hold it together. Bridget imagined the words of inspiration or bible verses Mae would recite aloud as a comfort. Oh sure, Mae had her dark moments. Bridget had first witnessed her weakness during the divorce. But she quickly pulled herself together and moved on without looking back. Bridget yearned for that courage, that faith in humanity and God to move forward with her life. She was making the effort, but a piece of her still remained in the past.

Ash Wednesday brought about an unusually cold, wet day. Once again, forecasts were calling for the possibility of freezing rain and icy conditions overnight. The coffee shop buzzed with conversations about the bizarre winter weather. Bridget's phone chirped with a text message. Schools were closed until Friday. Eli and Grace could barely contain their excitement. Bridget was glad for an extra day too. She was exhausted and dreaded facing a classroom filled with lively children.

She placed an order for hot chocolates for the kids and white chocolate mochas for herself and Mae. Eli and Grace picked two small tables by the window. Mae and her daughters entered the

Coffee House. Bridget waved to get her attention. Mae held her phone up displaying the text message and did a little happy dance before she hugged Bridget. Mae sat and scrolled through vacation photos on her phone and told Bridget all about the sights. The kids were at the next table chatting about not having school. Then the question came. "Well, Bridget, did I miss anything while I was gone?"

Bridget took a sip of her coffee and sighed heavily. "Actually, there is something I need to tell you. I didn't want to ruin your vacation, so forgive me for not letting you know sooner."

Mae looked worried. "Bridget, my goodness, you're scaring me. What's wrong?"

"I'm okay. It's Evelyn." Tears filled her eyes. She grabbed a napkin to keep them from falling down her cheeks. She cleared her throat and kept it together as best she could. "Evelyn got sick at work last week and was taken to the hospital. We all thought it was the flu or just plain exhaustion from working too much. Her test results showed that she has ovarian cancer. She had surgery on Monday to remove the tumor and the ovaries. It's moved into the surrounding lymph nodes. Dr. Monroe seems to think its stage three or worse. She's going home later today. She'll start treatment in a few weeks. Only time will tell if it's successful."

Mae gasped. "Oh dear Lord, no. Poor thing. I can only imagine what she's going through. You know, I went to the store before our trip, and she was our cashier. I noticed that she looked very worn down and tired. But like you, I thought she was coming down with something. I mean, so many people have the flu and pneumonia right now with this insane weather. How are Jack and the kids handling the news?"

"They are hanging in there for now. The kids have been staying with us. They went to the hospital with Jack this morning to visit Evelyn. They seem to be fine for the most part. Of course, they're a little young to understand the severity of her condition. And, Jack isn't telling them how serious things can get. I'm not sure I agree with that, but then again I don't know what I would do in his situation. I'm a nervous wreck. I just don't know what to do or say. I cleaned her house yesterday and made her bedroom cozy with flowers and candles, but it seems so trivial. Every time I'm with her, I just want to cry, scream, and curse. I don't want to upset her, but it's so unfair!"

Mae leaned across the table for Bridget's hand. "It's going to be hard. There are no magic words or deeds. We just have to be there for her, pray for her, and just be her friend. We have to believe that there is a reason for this, and God will get her through it."

Bridget chuckled. "Mae, you always know what to say. How do you do it? How do you stay so positive and faithful after everything you've been through? You should be so angry. It's been ten years since I lost Noelle, and I'm still ticked! What do you know that I don't know? Help me understand."

Mae thought for a moment. "Oh, I'm still mad at my ex-husband. I have good days and bad. But you can't let the negative take over your life, or it will destroy who you are inside. I learned that from my counseling sessions. You just have to move on and look for new beginnings. It's not easy, mind you, but it's necessary for your sanity and happiness.

And I know you miss Noelle. I was there, remember? But honey, you have to let her go. She's in Heaven, happy and watching over you. She wouldn't want you to hold on to her so tightly. Love her, remember her, and honor her memory, as you did with your grandmother. Letting go doesn't mean you forget. It means you've accepted loss. You'll see her again. It's just not your time yet, so please don't leave me. Who would go antiquing with me and help me pick out all those shoes?"

Bridget wiped away her lingering tears and laughed. Mae was right, just as she had always been. She was glad to have her friend back. They finished up their coffee and headed to the antique shop and bookstore for a little retail therapy. Bridget and Mae picked up a few new books for Evelyn's homecoming. They would visit her together tomorrow if the roads weren't iced over. Later that afternoon, they headed to church for mass and received the traditional ashes on their foreheads. Father John talked about the approaching Easter season and the opportunity to repent, reflect, and forgive. It was a time to reconnect with Jesus. All one had to do was ask. Bridget soaked up his sermon as if it was meant for her alone. When she was ready, she would ask.

As they exited the church, Bridget caught a glimpse of Joe and his grandmother across the parking lot. She was delighted to see him at church. The next time she saw him, Bridget would tell him how proud she was of his attempt to establish a relationship with God. Perhaps she still had a few good lessons left in her. Apparently, Joe had thought so anyway.

Before leaving, Bridget pulled her phone out of her purse to text Paul. He had to work late at the construction site to cover materials and equipment from the impending icy weather. She was letting him know that they were on the way home. Bridget quickly looked at her text messages to see if Jack had sent any updates about Evelyn's homecoming. Suddenly, a photo of Gloria appeared on the screen. Bridget had seen the same photo for months at the most opportune times. She couldn't help but giggle. "Welcome back, Gloria. I've missed you."

Chapter 13

HOMECOMING

Icicles hung from the gutters and a blanket of ice covered the ground and trees as far as the eye could see. No snow had fallen, which disappointed every kid in town, but a day off from school had made up for it. A fire roared and crackled in the living room. Paul had set up a tent for Eli and Grace last night. They were sad to see Kate and Kade go back home, so a pretend camping trip was just the thing to perk them up. Breakfast, of course, consisted of s'mores and hot chocolate. Blue and Rudy snuggled against the children and made sure they got their share. During the cold winter nights, Sidney had spoiled the pets rotten and gave them a taste for roasted marshmallows. Naturally, a special treat was roasted just for them.

Bridget turned on the television to watch the morning news. Road closures were widespread in the area, and people were encouraged to stay off the roads until the ice melted. Temperatures weren't expected to rise much above freezing, so the ice was to stick around for most of the day. The kids were crossing their fingers for another day off. Uncle Sidney quickly busted their bubble and announced that temperatures would be in the forties by morning. The bus would be here on time for sure.

Bridget knew the roads were too dangerous for traveling today. It was just as well. Evelyn probably needed rest and not a house full of company. After school tomorrow, she would check in on her friend. She was planning on cooking a huge pot of corn and crab soup tonight. She would set some aside for Evelyn's family. She thumbed through her cookbooks, looking for supper ideas that would be healthy alternatives for Evelyn. In the dessert section, she came across a coconut cake recipe that her cousin Beth had passed along years ago. She had made it for Evelyn's birthday last November. It was her absolute favorite dessert. Bridget would make her a cake this weekend. It might not be extremely healthy, but a little something sweet wouldn't hurt.

Bridget texted Evelyn to check in and told her not to bother with supper for tomorrow night. Also, she told Evelyn that Mae was aware of her situation and would call on her soon. She reminded her friend to call if there was anything she wanted or needed. She ended the text with words of encouragement and love. A feeling of guilt came over her as soon as she hit send. She wanted to call and hear Evelyn's voice, but she was still too shaken up. How did Evelyn's life come to this?

An hour later, Evelyn replied. She apologized for not texting sooner, but she had been asleep. She thanked Bridget for the clean house and relaxing touches in her room. Jack appreciated the offering of soup, which was one of his favorites. She reassured Bridget that she was doing okay. Jack's parents were flying in on Sunday. She would have many relatives keeping her company during the days ahead. She told Bridget that she loved her and appreciated her friendship. She ended the text reminding Bridget not to worry.

Bridget put the phone aside and began gathering the ingredients for the soup. She shook her head and wondered how she wasn't going to constantly worry about Evelyn. She vowed to pray every night for a speedy recovery and a miracle healing. Father John did say that the Easter season was a time for miracles. Maybe if enough people prayed for Evelyn, the cancer would respond to treatment and leave her with a chance for a normal life again. God had to listen this time. Bridget was determined that she would make him hear her again.

School reopened the next day, to the dread of students and teachers alike. Bridget struggled through the morning classes, trying to keep a smile for her students. Her mind was elsewhere, but it was Friday, so surely Bridget could survive one day before the weekend. During lunch, Mae and Bridget made plans to visit Evelyn after school. Mae's daughters would be with their dad for the weekend. Ann was picking up Eli and Grace for dental appointments, so the afternoon was theirs to visit a dear friend. Bridget was thankful to have Mae tag along. She would keep Bridget from falling apart.

At three-thirty, Mae and Bridget left the school parking lot together. Mae was stopping by her house first to pick up Evelyn's books and a cheesecake. Bridget ran home to get the soup. Mae was meeting Bridget so they could drive to Evelyn's together. Mae lived only two miles apart from Bridget. Evelyn's house was a bit further out of town by ten miles. She lived along a beautiful country road. It could be somewhat deserted at night, so for safety's sake, the two friends felt more comfortable as a pair.

Shortly after four o'clock, Bridget and Mae knocked on Evelyn's door with food and a gift in hand. Jack let them in and happily took the food to the kitchen. They went down the hall to Evelyn's room. She was up, watching her soap opera and fully dressed, makeup and all. Mae commented on how great she looked. Evelyn told them that she felt pretty good, too. She filled Mae in on her treatment plan. She told them that she intended on staying in town and allowing Dr. Monroe to handle her care. Although there were some excellent hospitals and doctors in nearby states, Evelyn and Jack felt as though this would be less traumatic for the children. She could come home to her family after each treatment. Dr. Monroe had many success stories, and he was up on the latest research. She had confidence in his abilities. Bridget and Mae agreed that she had made the right choice.

Moments later, Jack appeared with a tray of coffee and petit fours. He knew how much the three friends loved to chat over coffee and catch up on the latest gossip. Plus, the senior group at church had stopped by earlier to deliver all types of sweets for the family. Jack laughed and said someone had to help them eat it, or he would gain ten pounds!

The friends spent the late afternoon hours talking and laughing. Evening was approaching and daylight was fading. Bridget and Mae said their goodbyes. On her way out, Bridget told Jack that she would deliver a coconut cake on Sunday after church. Jack was delighted, hoping it would help Evelyn regain her appetite. Jack's parents were flying in from Virginia, so he asked Bridget if she would mind dropping off the cake around two and sitting with Evelyn while he drove to the airport. Bridget happily agreed. Since his parents would be visiting, Mae told Jack that she would fix a casserole for Sunday as well.

Bridget and Mae rode for a few moments in silence. Mae broke the silence and commented on Evelyn's positive attitude. "You know, attitude is half the battle. If you stay positive and have fight in you, then your chances of recovery are in your favor. Remember my Daddy's stroke and the long recovery he experienced? He never gave up. He made my life hell for a while, but he was hell-bent and determined to not let it get the best of him. I swear, that man is going to outlive me! That's the kind of perseverance Evelyn needs right now."

Bridget remembered all too well. She also recalled aloud to Mae her own grandmother's struggle with heart failure. "After her heart attack, Gloria was too weak and too far gone to fight. She just gave up. She was in pain and had been sickly for months on end. Even though we weren't ready to let her go, she knew it was her time. She had lived a long, happy life. But Evelyn is young. She has small children to raise. She hasn't lived a full life yet. Mae, it just seems unreal. It just makes you wonder sometimes what the man upstairs is thinking."

Rain softly began falling on the windshield. Winter had proven to be very wet and unusually cold. Mae complained about the weather and told Bridget that she was ready for spring. As they came around a sharp curve along the dark, country road, they noticed a car which had run off the road and into the ditch. It must have just happened because you could still smell burning rubber. Bridget pulled off to the shoulder, grabbed a flashlight from the glove compartment, and put her hazard lights on. Mae got out and immediately pulled out her phone to call 911, if necessary. The two carefully approached the car. It had run head on into a tree. The front end was smashed beyond recognition. Glass was shattered everywhere and the airbags had been deployed. Mae dialed 911 upon seeing the condition of the car.

Bridget went in for a closer look to relay information to Mae about the victim for the dispatcher. As she leaned into the driver's side window, she saw the driver covered in blood and slumped over on the steering wheel. She called to the driver a few times for a response, but no answer came. She gently took the driver by the arm to lean him back slightly for a closer look, trying not to move him too much to risk further injuries. She checked for a pulse. He was still breathing. She put her hand under his chin to turn his head slightly in her direction and shone the flashlight on him. She beheld a horrifying sight! Bridget dropped the flashlight and screamed. Mae ran over, phone in hand.

Bridget was as white as a ghost. Mae shook her and asked what was wrong. "Mae, it's Joe! The driver in the car is our former student, Joe!"

Chapter 14
Guarded Conditions

Sirens wailed in the distance. Bridget and Mae stood near the car, trembling with disbelief. They tried to get Joe to respond to them several times, but nothing worked. He was unresponsive. The best thing to do was wait for help and pray for Joe to be okay. The paramedics arrived on the scene. Joe had been training as a paramedic for months. He was well liked and respected by his peers. He had caught on rather quickly and had just started working full time with the crew. Rescuing someone close to you was never easy. This would be no exception.

Bridget and Mae spoke to the police officer on the scene. Bridget was assured that Joe's grandparents had been contacted about the accident. The paramedics had carefully laid Joe out on a stretcher. They were already working on him as they put him in back of the ambulance. Bridget ran over to ask them about his condition.

"How is he? Will he make it? I…I am a friend." Bridget could hardly make the words exit her mouth. Joe was young and had his whole life ahead of him. It was too soon for him to go.

A young lady, not much older than Joe, softly replied, "He's pretty bad off. He's lost a lot of blood and has a deep gash in his gut. He probably has some internal injuries and broken bones as well. In all honesty, it's up to God at this point. We are taking him to Lake Medical."

Bridget thanked her for the information. As soon as the ambulance left the scene, the friends got back in the car. On the way home, they discussed going to the hospital. Joe's grandparents were his only family. They would be there all alone to deal with paperwork, insurance, and doctors. Certainly, they would appreciate some help and two familiar faces. Bridget called Paul and filled him in on the accident. He encouraged her to go along to the hospital and asked her to keep him posted on Joe's condition.

Bridget and Mae met Joe's grandmother, Camille, in the emergency room. His grandfather was still at home recuperating from open heart surgery. She had called Joe's mother as a courtesy, but she had no interest in seeing her son. His father was in jail yet again on drug possession. Bridget thought to herself how pitiful Joe's family situation had become. What mother in her right mind would not care if her son lived or died? Regardless, Joe's grandmother seemed to be holding it together. She was grateful for Bridget and Mae's concern and help.

Joe was whisked away to surgery as soon as he arrived in the emergency room. Luckily, Elizabeth was working the night shift. She saw Bridget and inquired about Joe's accident. She reassured his grandmother that the doctor on call was an excellent surgeon.

Elizabeth would try to keep them informed on Joe's surgery. She offered to get them something from the cafeteria. Bridget and Mae hadn't eaten supper, so they took Elizabeth up on her offer.

Waiting rooms were hell on Earth. Bridget hated watching sick people come in and out. Worse yet, she hated seeing crying families being told horrific news about their loved ones. It was too depressing. Bridget had enough anxiety in her life to last her a lifetime. To lighten the mood, Bridget told a few stories to Camille about Joe's silly antics from second grade. Mae chimed in about his fourth grade year as well. Camille seemed to appreciate the distraction. A few of the ladies from her church group arrived to check on Joe. Camille was delighted to see so many of her friends.

Elizabeth came by an hour later to inform everyone that Joe was still in surgery and had no complications as of yet. The surgery was winding down at this point, so perhaps another hour at best until the doctor would be by to discuss his condition. Camille thanked her. The doctor appeared forty-five minutes later. Joe had made it through the surgery and would be in the ICU for at least the next twenty-four hours for observation. He had four broken ribs and a broken leg. He also suffered a serious tear in his spleen, which had to be removed. His forehead was covered in stitches, and he had a concussion. Joe was still unconscious, but he was lucky to be alive. He wasn't out of the woods, but the doctor was hopeful for a full recovery. His grandmother was the only one allowed to see him tonight, but only for a brief moment because Joe needed rest. Bridget and Mae bid Camille goodnight and told her that they would check in on Joe in the next few days.

The weekend seemed endless, which was unusual for Bridget. Usually, she found it hard to cram everything in on her to do list in two days. Saturday morning was spent in the barn with the animals and cleaning the stalls. She then proceeded to bake Evelyn's coconut cake. As the cake cooled, Bridget swept the courtyard and had coffee with Uncle Sidney. Grace helped to occupy Bridget's mind by asking her to play beauty parlor, which was one of her favorite role play games. Eli requested a game of checkers. Somehow, the children sensed that she needed a distraction. Paul also knew a distraction was in order. He offered to take the family out to Bridget's favorite seafood restaurant. She appreciated the opportunity to skip cooking and agreed without hesitation.

At the restaurant, Bridget ran into one of Camille's friends from her church group. Joe was still in ICU recovering from the surgery, but he was doing better and was awake. He could have limited visitors for now, but he would be moved to a regular room on Monday. Bridget was thrilled to hear the encouraging news and texted Mae with the update. She reminded Mae that she would be at Evelyn's around two o'clock. Mae could bring her casserole by and visit for a bit until she had to pick up the girls.

Sunday morning involved church and brunch. Every Sunday after church, Bridget's parents and Uncle Sidney joined Bridget's family at the local diner downtown for a late breakfast. It had become a new habit since Bridget started attending mass again. She enjoyed the time together as a family. She needed that time now more than ever.

At one-thirty, Bridget loaded the coconut cake into her car and headed for Evelyn's house. The drive gave her some time to gather

her thoughts. The country road was beautifully bathed in sunshine. A few thin clouds crossed the blue sky. A gentle, crisp breeze swayed the leafless tree branches from side to side. Bridget opened the sunroof of her car to let in the fresh air. The sunlight warmed her cheeks and a feeling of peace came over her. Maybe there was nothing to fear. Maybe Evelyn would beat this awful cancer.

Right at two o'clock, Jack and the kids left for the airport. Bridget brewed a pot of coffee and cut two slices of cake. Evelyn had anxiously awaited Bridget's visit. She told Bridget that Dr. Monroe had been by yesterday and was pleased with her progress. She had an appointment scheduled during next week. If all looked well, then treatments could begin in two weeks.

"Dr. Monroe said the treatments would take hours to complete." Evelyn explained. "How am I going to pass the time without going crazy? Jack can't spend that kind of time away from work twice a week. Mom will take me most of the time. I know you have school, but do you think you could stop by now and then for a few hours after work and sit with me? I mean, I love my mother, but what do you talk about all day long with a sixty-five year old?"

Bridget chuckled, "I understand totally. And you don't even have to ask. I'd love to keep you company. We can work out a schedule. Now, you better eat that cake before Jack comes back. I know he loves this recipe."

Evelyn ate every bite. As they sipped their coffee, she looked a bit puzzled. Bridget asked her what was on her mind. She hesitated, but decided to get it off her chest. "Something's been on my mind. Do you remember the talk we had about my beautiful experience in Heaven during my surgery?" Bridget nodded. "Well, I've had another one. And don't look at me like I'm crazy. It's not the anesthesia this time. This experience was just as real as the last one. I was in Heaven again. The same angel came to me and guided me there. This time, I was reunited with some of my relatives. Oh, they looked so good! Everyone was perfect. They just glowed with youthfulness! They were so happy. An utter feeling of joy came over me while I was there with them. I had so many questions, but the angel told me that I could only know the secrets of Heaven upon my passing and acceptance into his kingdom. The angel said that knowledge and understanding was God's gift to us in his kingdom. I would need to have faith until then. Before leaving Heaven, the angel did say that I would be blessed with one more visit. During that visit, I would understand all. That's all the angel said, then poof, I was back in bed!"

Bridget smiled. She knew the first dream had given Evelyn so much hope and peace. Who was she to judge? In the face of one's mortality, Bridget could only fathom the thoughts going through one's mind. Evelyn was on overload with thoughts of dying from cancer. Again, Bridget was convinced that it was only natural for her to dream of such things. A part of her wanted to believe so badly. However, Bridget lived in reality. Her faith was still shaky. Not even a so-called vision of Heaven was convincing enough to make her let her guard down.

Chapter 15

Chain Reactions

School bells rang bright and early on Monday morning. Bridget hated Mondays and lived for Fridays. Despite it all, she was ready to get back into a routine. She had missed her students and couldn't wait to begin new units for the spring semester. Her day went on as any other school day, and when it ended, Bridget was happy that she had survived it without worries on her mind.

On Wednesday evening, Bridget and Mae dropped the kids off at church for religion class. They had the evening to themselves, so they decided to stop by the hospital to visit Joe. With a candy bouquet in hand, the two friends walked to his room. Joe was watching the latest episode of *CSI*, and Camille sat on a chair, concentrating on her knitting. When they saw Bridget and Mae, they happily greeted them and were grateful for the company.

Joe looked awful. He was covered in bruises and scratches. A line of stitches danced across his forehead. His leg was in traction, which caused Bridget to cringe. Joe must have seen her grimace. "It's worse than it looks, I promise. I think my ribs hurt worse than anything, believe it or not. The doctor said I'm lucky to have survived the crash. I guess I can deal with a little pain and inconvenience. It could be worse."

Bridget replied, "Yes, I suppose it could be much worse. We are just glad you are okay. Fortunately, Mae and I came upon your car at the right time. Your paramedic friends worked quickly to get you to the hospital. They took very good care of you." Mae inquired about the accident and what caused him to veer off the road and into the tree line.

"Well, I worked late that evening. An emergency call came in as I was about to leave. I volunteered to help, but the call took longer than expected. I was running late for my adult religion class at church. So, of course, I was speeding. When I came upon the curve, a young deer ran out in front of me. I slammed on the brakes and started skidding on the wet road. Everything else is a blur. Did I kill the deer? Did you see it at the scene?"

Bridget and Mae shook their heads. They had not seen the deer anywhere in sight. Apparently, Joe had saved its life, risking his own. His expression showed his relief. "You know, that deer might have saved my life, or so my grandma thinks. If the deer hadn't been there and caused the accident, then I could've been killed in another accident near the church. A log truck had lost its load right about the time I would've arrived at the church. Nobody was hurt, but a few minutes more, and I could've been squashed like a bug!"

The newspaper did have a story about the accident. The mess created quite a traffic jam on a Friday night. Neither friend had realized how lucky Joe really was after all. Bridget pondered how life's little turns caused chain reactions. Every split second decision affected the next. Life was funny and cruel that way.

The time to pick up the children was drawing near. Bridget and Mae hugged Joe and told him how happy they were for his safety. Camille walked them to the door and stepped out into the hallway. "Thank you ladies for your concern about Joe. He always did regard the two of you very highly. As a matter of fact, I want to thank you, Mrs. Bridget, for showing Joe the way to God. He told me the two of you met in the chapel, and you taught him how to pray. For years, I've been trying to get him to church. Funny how his second grade teacher finally got through to him. I knew that if Joe didn't make it out of surgery, he was saved and would be welcomed into God's kingdom. You don't know how much of a comfort that was to me. I hope wonderful, Christian ladies like both of you continue to be a positive influence on Joe. Lord knows he needs it."

On the walk back to the car, Bridget thought about what Camille had said about Joe. Was it really true that her influence was so great that Joe began a relationship with God? She wasn't sure, but Bridget felt proud of Joe's efforts to change his life. Now if only she could influence herself so easily.

Bridget was restless by week's end. Her mind raced in so many different directions. She had papers to grade, lessons to write, loads of laundry to wash, and a visit with Evelyn planned. She laughed at herself for fretting. Just last weekend, she had to find things to make the hours go by. However, Bridget put all else aside on Friday afternoon. Evelyn deserved her time and full attention.

Their visit was pleasant. Catching up over coffee resumed as normal. It was just what Bridget needed to unwind. Evelyn made no more mention of another heavenly vision, and Bridget was glad for it. Evelyn was also grateful for Eli and Grace's presence. Kate and Kade needed to laugh and play. They needed to be normal children for as long as possible. Jack could be heard yelling above them over the newest Wii game. Evelyn got tickled at his childlike behavior. Bridget felt really hopeful after their visit. It was if nothing had changed. Oh, if only it would last. Bridget knew all too well that as soon as her treatments began, life would be hell for them all.

Bridget began her Saturday with a horse ride with Grace. She felt free on a horse. Keeping company with a horse was like free therapy, a release of stress. Many times, Bridget told her innermost secrets to her horse, Buckeye, as she brushed his long mane. Buckeye didn't seem to mind. He never passed judgment, and he was a great listener. Bridget was convinced that he was half human. He would nod, nudge, and neigh at just the right moments, as if he understood her completely. Buckeye was indeed a special horse.

The rest of the weekend whizzed by. As a matter of fact, the following two weeks were a blur. Bridget stayed busy with school work and daily life at home. Evelyn would start treatments on Monday. Bridget had already promised to sit with her on Thursday after school. She was nervous about how she would react to seeing a vile poison being pumped into her friend's body, knowing the side effects. Sometimes the cure was worse than the disease.

Chapter 16
WAITING

Evelyn's first treatment went off without a hitch. However, as luck would have it, she stayed sick for the next two days. As soon as she felt better, it was time for round two. The night before, Bridget had packed a tote bag filled with magazines, playing cards, crossword puzzles, and her tablet. She had downloaded a few movies and some of their favorite TV shows just in case. Surely they would find a way to pass the time.

After school, Bridget arrived at the hospital with her tote bag to relieve Evelyn's mother from duty. Bridget checked her email and wanted to post a few photos of Eli training Blue on Facebook. Suddenly, Gloria's photo popped up on her phone again. Somehow she knew Bridget needed courage. She shook her head and mumbled a word of thanks to Gloria for always being there when she needed her.

Bridget walked into the room. Evelyn smiled as her mother left and remarked, "Thank goodness you're here! I love my mother, I do. But if I have to listen to one more story about who has this ailment and who won the bingo games at church, then I'm going to scream! Please sit and tell me something, anything interesting!" Bridget giggled. The two friends continued their evening laughing and catching up on life.

Evelyn's treatments continued for the next several months. She slowly lost her hair, but she remained in good spirits. Bridget and Mae had taken her shopping downtown at the vintage stores for the wildest hats. She refused to wear a wig. Bald was beautiful and less trouble. She had lost a good bit of weight as well. Treatments made her sick most of the time, so eating became less and less appeasing. Regardless, she kept fighting and was determined to take back her life.

Evelyn hit a milestone in her treatment plan, and Dr. Monroe was ready to schedule a scan to see how effective the chemotherapy had been. He was hopeful that the scan would show improvement. Bridget spent the weekend praying for good news. She begged God for healing. The entire town knew of Evelyn's cancer and had prayed for her to beat the odds. If God wasn't listening to Bridget, surely he would hear everyone else.

Agonizing days went by as Evelyn awaited the results from her scan. Waiting was always the hardest when your life or the life of someone else depended upon a doctor's findings. Bridget knew that feeling all too well. She had went through twenty-four hours of pure hell ten years ago. Bridget was finally pregnant after years of trying with no success. The baby was due in December. She followed doctor's orders to perfection. Despite it all, only a week away from passing the first trimester, she began feeling a pain that was not normal. The next morning, the ultrasound showed that the baby hadn't progressed past eight weeks. There was no tiny heartbeat. The sweet child was gone.

Paul agonized for weeks, not sure of how to comfort Bridget. She blamed herself for the loss. The doctor said it was just one of those things, but Bridget had decided that God had punished her for past sins. One of the teachers at school was a pastor's wife. She had gone through the same experience, not once, but twice. As she visited with Bridget one day after school, she suggested the idea of naming the baby. She felt that it helped bring closure and gave the baby an identity. Bridget instantly fell in love with the idea. She decided upon Noelle since the baby was due right around Christmas. Paul agreed the name was perfect. It did help to name the baby, but Bridget held onto the grief and guilt. Letting go of the anger would have saved her a decade of despair. With Evelyn's life in jeopardy, Bridget was slowly coming to the realization that life was too short to be wasted living in the past.

Evelyn's scan results were not as expected. Although the cancer had not spread, it had not improved either. Dr. Monroe suggested a more aggressive approach with some experimental medications. Evelyn was trying to look on the bright side of things. At least it hadn't spread further into other organs. She was willing to try whatever Dr. Monroe suggested, at least for the time being. She had informed her family that when her quality of life suffered too greatly and treatment was only delaying the obvious, then she would accept her fate. Bridget hoped that Evelyn would never have to make such a choice.

Summer had finally arrived. The gloomy, cooler days gave way to warm afternoons and sunny skies. Wildflowers bloomed in vibrant colors. Uncle Sidney's hens and prize goat had brought about the excitement of babies to the barn. Eli and Grace were thrilled to tend to them. Blue loved to herd the baby chicks back to the barn each evening. Rudy watched with interest, but had enough mice to chase to entertain his time.

Bridget felt restless and full of energy. The beautiful weather and longer daylight hours meant spending more time outside. Uncle Sidney was pruning rose bushes again and cutting hydrangeas for a bouquet on the kitchen table. Paul and the kids were in the swimming pool, which Uncle Sidney had installed during the spring. He claimed the pool was to help him get some exercise, but Bridget knew better. With everyone occupied, she decided to take Buckeye out for a ride. The horse neighed with joy at the sight of his saddle.

Bridget and Buckeye went for a slow stroll through woods nearby. When they came upon the creek, Bridget stopped to give Buckeye a break. She led him to the shallow waters to drink and walked him to a shady spot under the trees. She pulled a few peppermints from her pocket and talked sweetly to him. Buckeye nodded and nudged her until she released the treat.

"Oh, Buckeye, I do love you. If only you could talk back to me and help me. You've listened to so many of my stories. I wonder if you get tired of me burdening you with my troubles. What's a girl to do?" He nudged her again to pet his nose. "Buckeye, I need your advice. Let's see how good your tips are today. Hmm… should I feed you carrots at the barn?" The horse nodded. "Okay, next question, am I your favorite girl?" Again the horse nodded. Bridget got tickled. "Alright Mr. Smarty Pants, is Rudy a bad kitty?" The horse stood still. "Well, I've got one to stump you for sure. Are there horses in Heaven?" Buckeye paused as if in thought. He nodded and neighed with enthusiasm. "You silly horse, you're just playing with me. You don't know a thing I'm saying, do you?"

Bridget turned to untie his lead rope from the tree. He gave her a nip. "Hey, boy! What are you doing? Are you trying to tell me you aren't ready to go yet?" The horse shook his head. "Are you saying you understand me?" Buckeye nodded. "So, there are horses in Heaven?" He nodded. "You must have heard me or the kids talking about Heaven." The horse was still. Bridget was confused. All coincidental, she convinced herself. Then Buckeye laid his head on her shoulder as if to embrace her. She handed him one last peppermint. A bluebird sang sweetly from a branch above them, then it flew away toward the barn.

Bridget began sobbing. "Well, boy, you are much smarter than I am. If a horse can have faith, then I think it's time that I do too. But, God, I just don't understand why certain things happen to certain people. I suppose it's not meant for me to know what you do. I'm just so tired of running away from you! God, forgive a fool! Please help me find my way back to you. Forgive me for ten years of anger and doubt. Please take me back. I know I've kept you waiting. Please don't let it be too late!"

And just like that, Bridget's heart opened and let God back in to work his wonders. Her soul was renewed with faith and love for the Lord. She knew the future was uncertain, but she was willing to face it with God's love and grace. She would still have days of doubt and would falter like any other sinner. Absolute rendering of her heart and soul would take time and healing. But this time, she could turn to God again for strength. Bridget knew that God worked in mysterious ways. It was no surprise that a faithful horse showed her the way back home.

Chapter 17
One Last Vision

Evelyn had another scan at the end of June. Her treatments had been increased, as well as the medications. She had more bad days than good ones lately. Bridget was concerned that this might be a sign that the current round of treatments hadn't worked as hoped. The results had come in on a Friday. Evelyn texted Bridget and asked to see her that same afternoon. Bridget had so much anxiety about her friend's prognosis. If Evelyn wanted to see her in person, it was either really good or really bad news.

When Bridget arrived, Evelyn was in her bedroom. Candles were lit and jazz music played in the background. Immediately, Bridget's spirits lifted. It must be good news. Evelyn motioned for her to sit on the bed. Bridget asked how she was feeling.

"I'm dying. There, I said it. The treatments didn't work. The cancer still hasn't spread, but it's not getting better. Dr. Monroe said that I should continue the experimental medications, but at this point chemotherapy was up to me. I think my quality of life is more important."

Bridget gasped, "Oh, Evelyn, no! Please don't quit! I need you! We all need you!" Tears slid down her cheeks.

"I'm not totally giving up, but I am going to enjoy the life I have left. I'm going to celebrate and do things I've always dreamt of doing. That's why you're here, darling! We are going to plan a dream vacation!" Evelyn tossed cruise brochures across the bed to Bridget.

"A vacation, are you nuts? How in the world can you think of such a thing?" Bridget was beside herself.

"Well, why not? There are places this chick wants to see before death knocks on my doorstep. And you and Mae, my dear, are coming with me! I mean, you couldn't deny a dying woman's wish, now could you?" Evelyn snickered.

Bridget folded her arms. "I'm glad you find this funny. What does Dr. Monroe say about you traveling all over? It's not like you're in the best health right now. What if something happens? You aren't thinking clearly. It's not like you're dying tomorrow. We have time to travel."

Evelyn grabbed Bridget's hand. "No, honey, I don't have the luxury of time anymore. Of course, none of us know how much time we have left. Dr. Monroe says that I could have six months, six years…who knows. I just don't want to leave this Earth with regrets."

"Do the children know?" Bridget sighed heavily. Evelyn nodded. "I see. How are they taking the news?"

"Better than you are! They're young, so death doesn't mean much to them yet. I'm hopeful that they will remember me. Help them remember me, Bridget." Evelyn broke down. The two hugged and cried until Evelyn grabbed for the tissues and told Bridget that they were big babies and needed to stop acting like fools. They had a trip to plan.

After looking through tons of brochures, it was decided that a cruise to Alaska would be the trip of a lifetime. It was a destination on their bucket list. The trip planning was underway. Evelyn had a great travel agent. She would contact her in the morning to start looking at cruise dates in July. She would call Mae and discuss the details as soon as she solidified a few possible travel dates. Evelyn was whirling with excitement. Maybe a change of scenery would do her mind and body good.

The Alaskan cruise was set to sail the week of July fourth. Somehow, Evelyn had made it happen. With only a few days to pack, Bridget and Mae raced around town to grab travel necessities. The children were beyond thrilled to see whales, eagles, and snow-capped mountains. Mae had gotten her ex to pay for the girls' portion of the trip. She called it payment for pain and suffering and reminded him how easy she let him off. His new girlfriend was none too happy with him handing over so much money. However, Mae kindly reminded her that the sports car and boat, which they both loved, could become all hers with one phone call to her lawyer. Needless to say, Mae got what she asked for and then some.

Paul had received a bonus check from the outlet mall construction job for early completion. He wanted to put the money into savings to begin a house fund. However, he knew how much this trip meant to Bridget. There would be other bonus checks. The house hunting would be put on hold until next spring. Uncle Sidney had overheard the conversation. He went to his study and unlocked a safe. He pulled papers from a folder inside. He called them into his study and shut the door.

He confessed to eavesdropping on their conversation about a new house. He handed Bridget his will and asked her to read aloud provision number three. Bridget read the statement. "The physical estate of Sidney and Esther, including the home, barn, and acreage shall be bequeathed to Bridget and her children." Bridget read it again as if it were a mistake. "How can you give me your estate? It's too much. I can't accept that sort of gift. What about the other nieces and nephews? What will they say?"

Sidney explained that it was Esther's wish that she inherit the house and land. Bridget was the only one who truly showed an interest in the aging mansion. Esther knew that she would never let it fall into ruin. Her family's home would be preserved under Bridget's love and care. Sidney reassured her that the others would have an ample inheritance, but the house was all hers. Bridget and Paul sat stunned. Sidney reminded them of all the love they had brought into the house. It was half theirs already. So, there really was no need to ever move or house hunt again. Bridget tearfully hugged her uncle. "Thank you and Aunt Esther for such a wonderful gift. Thank you for trusting me with a piece of her family history. I promise I will love it and cherish it as much as she did." Sidney knew that she would indeed keep that promise.

Later that night as Bridget was packing the suitcases, Paul still couldn't believe the provision in Sidney's will. "It's like an answer to a prayer. No more worry over money for a house. The children will be taken care of as well. A giant weight has just been lifted from my shoulders. We still have to save mind you. This is a huge estate to maintain. Oh, life is good. Life is very good. We are truly blessed." Bridget agreed and continued packing. Paul rattled on and on about the train ride and the whale watching and gold panning excursions in Alaska. He was wound up tighter than a top. It was as if a year of stress had all oozed away. Paul was going to learn how to be free and live again too.

Cruising the Alaskan coast was so tranquil. Bridget found peace in God's beauty all around her. The children found joy in spotting the whales, eagles, and mountain goats with their binoculars. The Tracy Arm Fjord was majestic and breathtaking. It was the highlight of their trip. As Bridget and her family gazed at the icebergs and mountains, Bridget made one of the best observations of her life. "Alaska is so beautiful. Words just can't describe the wonders here. Alaska is the closest place to Heaven. It's like you are here with God. You can see his work everywhere in its greatest form. If God wanted us to see Heaven on Earth, then he succeeded. His perfection is all around us. If anyone ever questioned his existence, then this would be the place to convince a doubter otherwise."

It was chilly sitting on the deck, so Jack and Paul were sent to get hot chocolates for everyone. The children were busily playing with their binoculars and taking turns watching for wildlife. The naturalist on board was telling them about all the animals that lived in the fjord. Mae was taking photos with her new camera and chatting with an older gentleman about the sights. Evelyn and Bridget sat and took in the view.

Evelyn grabbed Bridget's hand. "Bridget, you know how much I love you, don't you?" Bridget nodded. "Your friendship has been one of the best gifts in my life. I have a gift for you in return. It's not a tangible gift. Call it a spiritual gift. I had another vision last night."

"Oh, really? Wait! Wasn't this going to be the last one before… before, you go?" Bridget questioned these visions, but she was concerned nonetheless.

"Yes, it was the last one. But, I'm not going yet, so don't panic! The angel didn't tell me when it was my time. She said that only God knows when our time is over. During this visit, we were alone in the garden. I didn't see my relatives, just my angel. She told me to be brave. God has great plans for me. She told me that God had given her a special assignment. He had chosen her to be my guide into Heaven. She would watch over me and bring me to meet God when my life is over. She hoped that her purpose in Heaven would give you purpose on Earth."

"Me? What does your vision have to do with me?" Bridget felt a chill run down her spine as an icy breeze blew around her.

"Bridget, the angel that has been my guide through Heaven is your daughter."

Bridget went pale. She stood up and walked over to the deck railing. She felt sick and confused. Evelyn followed her and stood beside her, looking out at the horizon. "I know this is hard for you to hear and even harder for you to understand. Believe me, I had a hard time with this myself. I am Noelle's special assignment. She told me that God chose her from the beginning of her life to help me into Heaven. She told me to let you know that she is happy and fulfilling God's plan for her. She wants you to live a good life with no regrets, Bridget."

Bridget ran her hands through her hair and paced back and forth. "How? How can I know this is real and not a crazy dream?"

Evelyn locked her arm around Bridget's. "Noelle said you would have doubts. So, she told me two stories to convince you that my visions are real. The first story is about your friend, Joe. God knew that Joe was going to die if he went further up the road the night of his accident. It was supposed to be his time, but God was so moved by his newfound faith and trust in him. God has a new plan for him. Joe is going to accomplish great things in God's name. Noelle was sent to change the course of events. She was the deer in the road."

Bridget had to grab hold of the rail to keep her knees from buckling. "Oh, my, Evelyn. There's no way you could know anything about the accident. Mae and I never told you the details. So, my daughter was the deer? How can she be an angel and a deer?"

Evelyn laughed, "Oh, darling you have a lot to learn when you get to Heaven. Angels take many forms. As a matter of fact, she was there the day you rode Buckeye into the woods. You asked Buckeye many questions that day, didn't you?" Bridget nodded. "You got the answers you needed from that old horse because Noelle was there too. She appears as a bluebird quite often in the barn. Buckeye and Noelle are good friends. God knew that Buckeye had to be his instrument, so Noelle was there to help Buckeye answer your questions. And it worked, I'm told."

Bridget wiped tears away. "Yes, it did. I've seen that bluebird so many times. I figured it had a nest in the barn someplace. All the time, it was her? Oh, I just don't understand!"

"Bridget, if Noelle hadn't died, Joe would be dead right now. She wouldn't have been there in the road to cause him to swerve into the trees. Maybe, just maybe, you saved his life too by talking to him about God and how to pray. You might not have had that chance if you hadn't been in the chapel, feeling sorry for yourself and me the day of my surgery. Joe's change of heart saved him. And, if she wasn't an angel, then I would have no guide into Heaven. No one would be there to give me strength. None of my visions would have taken place and given me a sense of peace and acceptance of my fate without her. So, you see, God had a plan for Noelle all along. Her death had a purpose. I'm honored that she is my angel. You gave me a precious gift."

Both of them were crying, trying not to attract attention to themselves. "Evelyn, what does she look like? I've always wanted to know what she could've become. I always had a sense that Noelle was a girl. I can't explain it, just a feeling I guess. I'm glad that my instincts were right. Please tell me anything you can about her."

"She's beautiful. Blonde, curly hair, blue eyes like Paul's, fair skin, and the most beautiful lavender wings! I don't know her age, but she just glows with a light unexplainable."

"Lavender wings? That's funny. Gloria said that she wanted purple wings when she got to Heaven. She also said that she saw angels during her last few days on Earth." Bridget got choked up. "Evelyn, you don't suppose the angel Gloria saw was Noelle, do you?"

"Noelle didn't say a word about Gloria, but I wouldn't be surprised that she was there along with Gloria's chosen guide into Heaven. It's unbelievable, isn't it? But, God has given both of us a wondrous gift! It's so ironic how one life touches so many others. Thank you for being a part of mine."

The two embraced until they saw the kids running back up the stairs with hot chocolate in hand. They wiped each other's makeup smeared faces and put on smiles for their families. As she sipped her hot chocolate, Bridget decided to edit some of the photos which she had taken with her cell phone. When they arrived in Skagway tomorrow, she would post their adventures on Facebook for her family and friends to see. Out of the blue, who appeared on her phone? Why, Gloria, of course! She had done it again. She was always there to watch over Bridget. Why would Alaska be any different? Apparently, she wanted to let Bridget know that she was there on the trip of a lifetime, too. Or maybe it was her way of letting Bridget know that she was fine and Noelle was with her, as suspected. Either way, Bridget was happy to see her smiling face.

Later that night, Bridget shared Evelyn's vision with Paul. He was just as moved. Bridget admitted that she had taken her life and blessings for granted. That was over for good. From that point forward, Bridget was whole again. She never lived another day with regret.

Chapter 18

Goodbyes

Summer was coming to an end. Bridget and Mae were back at school working in their classrooms, getting ready for another group of students. School would start in two weeks, and Bridget could hardly believe how quickly time passed. Evelyn had stopped the chemotherapy. She had accepted the time she had left and was able to maintain an almost normal life. People who didn't know any better would have never guessed that she was dying of cancer. Dr. Monroe had not given her a definite timeframe. He was a Christian man and believed that this knowledge rested with one man alone. Who was he to tell someone when their life would be over? He wanted her to live each day as her last.

Speaking of the good doctor, Mae had caught his attention. Evelyn had introduced them on several occasions, and apparently, Dr. Monroe had been quite spellbound with her gentle spirit. After a Labor Day BBQ at Evelyn's house, he took the plunge and asked her for a date. The two became inseparable. It was no surprise that by the holidays, the two were engaged. A June wedding was in the works. Bridget and Evelyn couldn't have been more pleased.

As months rolled by, Bridget, Mae, and Evelyn continued their trips to the Coffee House and the mall and arranged play dates with the kids as usual. Evelyn was filling up her calendar with all sorts of fun outings and trips for her family and friends. She had taken Dr. Monroe's advice to heart. She was living to the fullest. Over many coffee filled afternoons, they shared photos from their many adventures together. Evelyn was putting a scrapbook together for Kate and Kade. It would be a special, priceless gift to them upon her passing. Unbeknownst to everyone, including Bridget, Evelyn was also writing goodbye letters to her dearest friends and to her beloved Jack. Each letter contained her words of wisdom, memories, and her wishes for them to go on with their lives until they all reunited someday. Throughout their lives, those exact letters would be read over and over again until they were tattered and torn. Evelyn would never be far away.

Autumn had settled in for another year. Bridget sat on the courtyard with Paul, enjoying the cool air. She recollected the previous fall season when her life was so unsettled. She was like a leaf being tossed by the wind with no direction, no purpose. She was so proud of how far she had come since then, both spiritually and emotionally. Her life wasn't perfect. There were still some obstacles to overcome, and she had sad days once in a while. But, the sadness wasn't controlling her any longer. The dark storm clouds had blown over and the sun shined again in her soul.

Seasons quickly changed. The holidays were on the horizon once again. Only, this holiday season would be the most joyous of Bridget's life. She had a new relationship with God and with herself. She no longer had to pretend for anyone's sake, including her own.

Christmas brought about the usual excitement and anticipation. Decorations exploded in every nook and cranny with Bridget's new Christmas spirit. As the tree was being trimmed, Paul presented her with a small, red velvet box. He said it was an early Christmas gift. Bridget joked and told him that he would have to wait for Santa to bring his gifts. There would be no peeking until his arrival. Bridget opened the box and inside was a delicate glass ornament. She lifted it slowly. It was a bluebird. Paul had remembered the story of the bluebird and Buckeye. Bridget hugged him.

"Thank you for remembering. Thank you for the wonderful life you've given me. It took me long enough to realize it, but I am beyond blessed. All I ever needed was always right here in front of me. You and the children, including our angel, are my greatest gifts, my greatest accomplishments in life." Bridget kissed him on the cheek and turned toward the tree. She hung the bluebird on one of the highest branches to remind her to look up and thank God for making Noelle a part of her life.

Christmas Eve had arrived. The children were anxiously waiting for the traditional exchange of one gift from under the tree. Eli and Grace tore through the wrapping paper and discovered pajamas and slippers with their favorite Disney characters. Inside the slippers was a note for each of them from Santa. He was giving them a trip to Disney World after Christmas! Eli and Grace screamed and jumped up and down. Evelyn had made the trip a special request from old St. Nick. One last hoorah.

After the utter chaos had calmed, Eli and Grace gave Paul and Bridget the gifts that they had made for them at school. Bridget had kept every single one of them since preschool. Each year, she displayed the precious gifts in her china cabinet. Eli had made a gingerbread ornament for the tree and a Popsicle stick bird feeder. He told them that the seeds inside should get the bluebird in the barn to come back. Bridget and Paul exchanged a smile. It was Grace's turn. She had made a pinecone Christmas tree and had a drawing tied up with a string. The drawing had a snow-capped mountain in the background with blue skies. Three angels stood at the foot of the mountain. Grace explained that one was Miss Mae. She had the blue dress and pink high heels and pink wings. The next angel was Mrs. Evelyn. She had on a green dress with yellow wings and flip flops. Mrs. Evelyn loved her flip flops!

"The angel in the middle is you, Mommy. I put you in the middle so you could be by both of your BFFs. See the mountain in Alaska?" Grace pointed out the details.

"Yes, Grace, it's lovely. Why put angels in Alaska? Did you see one while we were there?"

"No, silly! You said that Alaska was the closest place to Heaven. So I put you, Miss Mae, and Mrs. Evelyn there as angels cause that's what we are all gonna be one day, you know."

Bridget grinned. "I see. You are so right. I love your picture Grace, but I think it's missing something. Where are my shoes and wings?"

Grace leaped up. "Wait right here! I'll be right back!" Grace came back in a few minutes carrying her crayon box. "I waited for your shoes and wings so that they would be just right for you. So, what kind of shoes do you want in Heaven, Mommy?"

Bridget thought for a moment, going through her shoe collection in her mind. "I'll take my favorite pair of red cowgirl boots please." Grace carefully drew red cowgirl boots onto Bridget's feet.

"Ok, now it's time for the angel wings. What color wings would you like?" Bridget dug a crayon out of the box. She didn't have to think about it at all. She already knew the perfect color for her wings. She handed Grace the crayon.

"Make my angel wings purple, please!"

EPILOGUE

Bridget's personal battle with her faith and relationship with God is something most of us can relate to on some level. We've all been tested in different ways. We've all had trials and tribulations in our lives. How we overcome those challenges make us who were are today. Faith is hard. If it was easy, then none of us would want to pursue it. Faith can falter or be reaffirmed with each new event in our human lives. God knows our strengths and weaknesses, our triumphs and our defeats. He is there to lift us up in our darkest hours and rejoice with us in times of joy. We just have to be willing to open the door and let him in.

Evelyn lost her battle with cancer in the spring. But her faith brought her through her darkest hours and allowed her to accept her fate and live each day as her last. And you can bet that Noelle was holding her hand at her last dying breath. Angels are all around us every day. Only, we get so busy and caught up in the daily grind of life that we often miss their presence. If we slowed down and stopped to listen more carefully, we would all find God speaking to us more clearly.

Mae did marry Dr. Monroe the following summer. It was a beautiful outdoor ceremony by the lake. Although Evelyn was not there in body, Bridget and Mae knew that she was there in spirit. Yellow roses from Evelyn's garden were used in Mae's bouquet. A single yellow rose was placed on a chair next to Jack. Her seat had been reserved months ago. During the reception, Bridget and Mae spotted two bluebirds singing in a tree nearby.

Joe made a full recovery after his accident and went on to have a successful life. He married a paramedic…the young lady at the scene of his accident. As a wedding gift, Bridget gave Joe a painting by a local artist that depicted a young deer in the woods. The inscription on the back read, "Nothing in life happens by accident. Love, your favorite second grade teacher, Mrs. Bridget." Joe and his wife work at the church two nights a week counseling teenagers about their faith. Joe had lived up to God's expectations. He is doing great things in God's name.

And last but not least, there's Bridget. Evelyn's death was hard, but Bridget stood in the cemetery, comforted by the fact that her friend was in Heaven with her daughter as her faithful, loving guide. Her relationship with God grew stronger with each passing day. He had offered her an insight into his heavenly purpose for Noelle through Evelyn's visions. That was a gift she was to never forget. She only shared those visions with Paul and Mae at first. But both encouraged her to share her amazing story with others. Her experiences might bring others joy, understanding, and comfort. Best of all, others could find their way back to God through her inspirational tale.

Bridget did decide to share her personal story. She became a great motivational speaker at Christian conferences all over the world. However, her schedule revolved around the school year because she remained a second grade teacher. Kids like Joe kept her grounded and reminded her of the lessons that she still had to teach.

Once in a while, that little bluebird visited the barn to check on Buckeye. Sometimes the bluebird came alone or with several others. Bridget was never sure if that bluebird was Noelle or just coincidental. But she liked to imagine that it was indeed her daughter along with Evelyn, Gloria, Esther, and many others just stopping by to say hello from Heaven.

When the time would come for Bridget to go home, she was certain of two things. First, she would not be alone. God would welcome her into his kingdom, and she would spend an eternity getting to know and love her lost child. Second, when she got to Heaven, Bridget would be walking the gardens of God's kingdom in her red cowgirl boots and flying through the air with spectacular, purple wings.

A copy of Grace's drawing of the three angel friends is brought along with Bridget during every motivational speech. She shares it with her audiences to end her incredible story. Grace's priceless work of art hangs in Bridget's foyer to this day as a constant reminder of God's great, unconditional love.

Bridget hopes her story has strengthened your faith, lessened your doubts, and inspired you to grow in God's grace as time goes by.

Be of good courage, and he shall strengthen your heart, all ye that hope in the Lord. (KJV, Psalm 31:24)

The End

Acknowledgements

Writing this book was not an easy task. So many issues in Bridget's life are somewhat my own. God, however, inspired me and guided me through the pages so that I may share my story with you. I give God and my special angel in Heaven the credit for this story.

None of this would be possible without the love and support of my family and friends who believed in my dreams and encouraged me daily to use my God-given talents.

Thanks to my husband, Kevin Woods, for being my rock and for always allowing me to follow my heart's desires. Thanks for being a wonderful father and Christian role model for our children.

My children, Caleb Paul and Abbygale Grace, have been my greatest accomplishments in life. Thank you for being my hardest critics!

For my parents, Armand and Jean Duhe, words cannot express the gratitude that I have for the life lessons you taught me. Much thanks to my sister, Brandy Duhe Martin, who always has my back in good times and bad.

Kimberly Dawn Threeton and Gabrielle Lambert Page, my Mae and Evelyn, the two best friends anyone could ask for in life. I cherish our friendship. Kim, thanks for keeping me grounded. Gabrielle, thanks for bringing out my adventurous side.

Laura White Williams was my first unofficial editor ten years ago when I began my writing obsession. Thanks for pushing me to keep writing.

For Dave and Phyllis Monaret, my greatest uncle and aunt on the planet, thanks for filling my life with love and laughter.

Julian and Marvell Woods, my in-laws, who have loved me like a daughter and tolerated my whimsical ways.

Honor goes to those who have lost their battle to cancer or struggle with this disease everyday, namely Kim Capdeboscq, Terry Lobell, Whitney Borne, and Evelyn Cano. May you rest in God's loving arms.

Book Club Discussion Questions

1. Bridget spent ten years turning away from God because of the loss of her child. Have you ever experienced a loss that affected your faith? If so, how did you overcome your grief and maintain your faith in God?
2. Bridget and Paul both experienced the loss of Noelle. However, Paul's coping mechanisms differed greatly from Bridget's. Explain or discuss the similarities and differences between how men and women handle loss and grief.
3. Joe was Bridget's former second grade student. Her influence on his life continued into his young adulthood. How did Joe's respect for Bridget change his life? Do you have a hero? How did he/she change your life or faith in a positive way?
4. At one point in the story, Evelyn tells Bridget that she is the best medicine. Discuss how positive friendships/relationships help us face daily life. How can negative relationships, like Joe's relationship with his parents, damage our faith and outlook on life?

5. What were some of the turning points in Bridget's journey back to her faith?
6. Evelyn has visions of an angel. Do you believe in angels and their ability to watch over us? Why or why not?
7. If you had a non-believer, like Joe, approach you about your faith in God, what kind of testimony or advice would you offer to convince them God exists?
8. Bible verses often give us a sense of comfort. What is your favorite verse? Why is it so meaningful to you?
9. During the story, we discover Joe's accident was no accident at all. A deer standing in the road saved him from death. Do you believe that nothing in life happens by chance? Can you name a time in your own life when a twist of fate changed the course of events?
10. Evelyn's visions of her angel, Noelle, convince Bridget once and for all of God's purpose, mercy, and love. Without those visions, Bridget might not have fully given her heart to God. We all can't receive such direct messages from God, but God is speaking to us daily. How do you communicate with God? What time of day do you devote to talking to God? Do you have a favorite prayer or devotional that you can share?

Contact Me:

I would love hearing from you and reading your stories of inspiration! Feel free to follow me on Facebook (Wendy D Woods Book Club) Twitter, and Instagram (#louisianaauthor).

God bless you,

Wendy

CPSIA information can be obtained at www.ICGtesting.com
Printed in the USA
LVOW12s1549240215

428126LV00001B/69/P